Dusty Foot Philosophers

By

Ayanna D. Gouch

Roots of Sapphire Press

Detroit, MI

Roots of Sapphire Press

Cover Design by Ed Royster

Dusty Foot Philosophers/ Ayanna D. Gouch

Ebook: ISBN 978-9589912-0-3

Paperback: ISBN 978-09859912-1-0

http://www.ayannadevan.com

To my family who raised me, supported me, guided me and let me find my own way. You are my daily motivation and inspiration.

To my friends who are more like extended family, our bonds are unbreakable and I am forever grateful for having you in my life.

To my students who brighten my day with your youthful energy. You have shown me the true meaning of what it is to be a dusty foot philosopher.

Table of Contents

Playlist

Kick, Push / 7

Lost in the World / 19

The Show Goes On / 23

Golden / 34

Daydreamin / 38

Out My Mind, Just In Time / 52

All of the Lights / 60

Fallin / 66

Flashing Lights / 72

Runaway / 82

Empire State of Mind / 86

Thugz Mansion / 103

If I Ain't Got You / 111

Gone Til November / 118

Get It Together / 125

Headed in the Right Direction / 136

Pressure / 147

The People / 155

Sex 4 Suga / 163

Didn't Cha Know / 168

The Coolest / 176

Butterfly / 191

I Keep / 208

Ready for Love / 226

I Used to Love Him / 242

Foreword

Children are the hope for the future of mankind, treat them with respect, love them wholeheartedly, listen to their thoughts, and expect the same from them. Nurture their bodies with fruits and grains from the earth and their minds with the ancient wisdom of our ancestors. Promote peace and tranquility through meditation. Thus, equality, productivity and sustainability will follow close behind an intellectual race with intuitive sensibilities.

I wrote the above paragraph one day when I was trying to pull together the general takeaway message of this book. It may seem at times that the lives of the main characters are quite turbulent. Drama, however, was not really the goal. Every sentence in this novel is a part of a bigger picture, a unified message of health and wellness. Historically, black people in America have endured many traumatic experiences and it is simply impossible to right the wrongs of economic, political and social degradation through the acquisition of money and power. These two, combined especially, have proved to be more of a hindrance in our communities than a means for collective prosperity. A spiritual awakening is certainly in order. The lives of Sasha, Devontae and Nawiri tell a story of modern day experiences. It is a mixture of realism and idealism, as I've tried to reveal some things I have seen and some things I would like to see more of. In the spirit of love and communal healing, I invite you to read my first novel with an open mind and open heart. Thank you.

KICK, PUSH

Summer was the time of frolic and play, when swings were in constant motion and playscapes came alive. The bright sun reflected off the necks of perspiring children, who only went for water when it was no longer resistible. Daylight savings time had yet to shorten the days but the fun was now limited to the early afternoon because school was scheduled to start in only three and a half short days.

On September 2, 1999, five hundred children entered Century Academy, a Junior High School for seventh through ninth graders. They had stuffed clean, crisp notebooks, sparkle gel pens, colored pencils and fresh erasers into green, blue, purple and pink backpacks. Looking at their supplies, they were ready to get to work but their apprehensive attitudes showed that they would have much rather been playing basketball or chasing after ice cream trucks. Mrs. Ecko's homeroom class filed in, taking seats by their friends and bffs (best friend forevers), chatting, cracking jokes on other's uniforms and paying little attention to her stern expression.

Mrs. Ecko cleared her throat, 'Uhmm, good morning class, welcome to the eighth grade! This is a year of TRANSFORMATION, you will either learn to swim or you will drown in work. Which one will YOU be – a drowner or a swimmer?' She said with large, frightening eyes. 'I have seen many a bright-eyed students, smiling and laughing their way into this classroom at the beginning and crying on their way out. So make sure you don't fall behind, fall asleep or fall for any of these knuckle head BOYYYSSS in here. Yes ladies, I'm talking to you. As you know, I am not only your homeroom teacher but I am also your English and Social Studies instructor, so we will be spending loads of quality time together this school year!'

The children looked around at one another with sideways glances. Not knowing what to expect always made the first few days of school awkward and terrifying at times. Mrs. Ecko was a gentle and kind-hearted woman as the students would soon learn but now was the time for the classroom rules to be ingrained into their impressionable minds. Classroom rule number one: construct systems to counteract all tendencies for precocious behavior.

Kahira raised her hand, 'Miss Ecko, what exactly is social studies? I mean I'm already social, so I don't see why we gotta study it. I know social, I could even teach you a few things about being social.' The class chuckled.

Mrs. Ecko responded, 'Well, social studies is more than just the study of personal interactions, it also investigates general social trends in a country such as fashion, current events, the economy, politics, migration, white supremacy, social theories and more. I believe you are referring more so to the social interactions between individuals which certainly plays into the bigger picture. In fact, the behavior and mannerisms of children in a society are a direct reflection of the social environment in which they are raised, which in today's world includes the influences of the media on your MINDS! And of course you know more about your mind than I do. So, perhaps we can learn from one another, how does that sound?' Mrs. Ecko asked with raised eyebrows.

She could tell the kids were impressed by her rcsponse, she was expecting to be tested for the first few weeks of class. 'The students want to see how much I can handle,' she thought, 'and they'll see I'm the one who throws the curve balls around here.' She recognized one of her students, whom many teachers acclaimed as extremely astute and an overall high achiever. They said she could give a coherent and well thought answer within seconds, so Mrs. Ecko was secretly looking forward to observing this young lady's talent for herself. Perhaps the hype was exaggerated – only time would tell.

The student's name was Nawiri Simmons. She wore thick bifocal glasses, with many twists in her long black hair. Her skin was the color of mahogany, her eyes were bright, teeth covered by clear braces and her frame was thin and fragile. While her beautiful features often went unnoticed by others, many classmates never failed to tease her about various flooding uniform slacks that were never quite long enough to cover her shoes, so she was given the unflattering nickname 'Flood.' Throughout elementary school, she begged her grandmother to buy her longer school pants but Ms. Heath refused because she did not understand her granddaughter's embarrassment and was more concerned about saving money for Nawiri's college education.

'Nawiri, your pants look fine, young people shouldn't be so concerned with appearance, you're sole purpose is to learn in school, not to look cute!' Appealing to her mother had proven to be just as useless, as her mother was only concerned with her own appearance. So, she started saving up funds, industriously, from her summer lemonade stands and weekly allowances to buy new slacks for herself. Nawiri sat with Sasha Gordon, who had been her closest friend since the 2nd grade. Now, they were more like sisters; very competitive in school but could always put schoolwork aside to talk on the phone and hang out on the weekends.

Tim Johnson sat across from them; he was the proclaimed class clown. Infamous around the school for his trickster techniques and clever ways of secretly making fun of the teachers in front of his classmates. In fifth grade, he stood behind the Ms. Calwell for close to three minutes imitating her every move as she disciplined the class. She only found him there as she moved backwards to pick a piece of chalk from the board and heard the yelp from the young man behind her whose foot was caught under her stiletto heel. Tim sat with his athletic friends, who dominated the recess court with their football and basketball games - each of their faces twitching with excitement for the basketball team tryouts in the afternoon.

The 'popular girls' sat in the corner, near the metal file cabinets. They were constantly whispering and giggling, occasionally glancing over at the athletes, and sharing their pink and red Lip Smackers glitter glosses. To Nawiri, they were perfect, life size Barbie Dolls with thoughts of clothes, shoes, boys, parties, sex, boys, hair, skin, boys, especially Tim and his friends. In fact, Kierra had just begun to tell her friends about an exciting idea, 'Guys! You know what I was just thinking? Hold on, I forgot. Oh right, what do you think I should do for my birthday? I think I want one of those big mirrors that come with a desk under it; I think it's called a fanity or manity, something like that. Oh, and I want to have a sleepover and a dinner at Red Lobsters, so that one of my boos – Tim or Emmanuel – can come but I haven't decided which one to invite yet. My mom says if I have the sleepover all the girls that come can get one hundred dollars for a shopping trip at Great Lakes Mall!' She leaned in closer, 'We might even be able to get our nails done!' With juicy secrets and desires revealed, the girls had much to discuss and plan for the rest of the day.

After roll call, the bell rang and the students dispersed for their first hour classes. Nawiri and Sasha headed to Algebra. They were each anticipating the best grades but kept their ambitions secret. Some of the other students from their homeroom were also headed to Algebra, many of them had never been in the same class as Nawiri, so she was anxious to see how smart they were and more importantly, if they could keep up with her and Sasha. Upon entering the room, they were surprised to see that an entire problem set had already been written on the black board.

'Dang!!! Look at all this stuff, I've never seen a letter in a number problem before!' Sasha declared. 'Me neither,' Nawiri replied, worried. Before Algebra, the most complicated math they had seen was order of operations and some word problems. In their eyes, this foreign combination of letters and numbers looked more like hieroglyphics than mathematics.

They sat at the front table, hesitantly opening their textbooks to find some quick explanation of the strange math that stared mockingly down at them from the board.

'Close those books!' exclaimed Mr. Edison. I can't have you girls getting a head start over the other students, we have to learn together and work through these problems collectively!' The students were quite frightened by his suspicious smile and Albert Einstein hairdo. These eighth graders had not mentally prepared themselves for such a challenging start to their first day back to school. The teachers seemed to be so stern, relentless and – CRAZY!!

There was one student in the class who showed no signs of fear or surprise. 'Who is that?' Nawiri asked Sasha, flashing her eyes in his direction. 'I think his name is Devontae. I hear he keeps to himself but that he does really well in school,' Sasha replied.

Nawiri was not impressed; she opened her notebook, still eyeing Devontae out of the corner of her eye. She was a born competitor; always scoping out the competition and vowing to show them up in one way or another.

'Ok class, for those of you who don't know me, my name is Mr. Edison and I am your eighth grade Algebra teacher. Unlike most other teachers, I like to jump right into the material on the first day of school, just to give you all a taste of what Algebra is all about and an idea of what is coming your way. Has anyone ever seen problems such as those listed on the board?'

Silence fell over the room but then from nowhere, Devontae raises his hand, 'I have.' Everyone turned around, surprised that anyone could answer yes, especially a scraggly kid like him. Judgmental, jealous eyes glared at him as he sat firm, slightly slouched, with his eyes directly on the teacher and no one else. He could feel their stares burning into his chest but he refused to acknowledge them with even a glance. The kids at Century irritated him, they showed little happiness for others; everyone seemed to be absorbed in their own personal pursuits for success or popularity. At his neighborhood school, there was more fighting and arguing but at least you didn't have to guess what people were thinking. At Century, everything was a mind game.

'Is that right? And where have you seen such problems?' asked Mr. Edison, intrigued.

'My neighbor gave me an Algebra book and I did some problems out of it last summer when I was bored and just chillin' around the house and shit,' Devontae replied, nonchalantly. His eyes were still glued on Mr. Edison, observing the shifts in his facial expressions from surprise, to doubt and finally to genuine curiosity.

'Ok, great! And by the way, please watch your language in my class.'

'My bad,' Devontae replied, embarrassed to have shown ill-manners on the first day.

The lesson continued and Nawiri was annoyed throughout the entire session. Devontae knew all the answers and everyone else, including her, was lost. 'This is not acceptable,' she thought. Tomorrow I'm coming back with the whole damn book memorized, we'll see how Mr. Devontae feels about that!' As a magnet school, most students were striving for excellence, whether it was self-proclaimed motivation or forced by their parents, they all at some point had the desire to shine. There were those, such as Nawiri, whose ego made it mandatory to excel and she would do so at any cost. Extra hours of study, practice – more study and more practice – to have advanced proficiency in everything was a worthwhile sacrifice of time in her eyes.

For the next two months, Mr. Edison's class became a tug-o-war for power and attention between Nawiri and Devontae. If Mr. Edison asked for a volunteer, their hands shot up without hesitation. They raced to complete assignments and Nawiri would look over her shoulder with an antagonizing smirk whenever she finished first. There was nothing friendly about this competition, only ambition turned pure malice drove them onward. They did all of this silently, without ever speaking a word to one another. Body language became key to their communication. From the straightening of a back, which meant Nawiri was about to finish the class work, to the breaking of a pencil lead when Devontae was struggling with a problem.

Toward the end of October, Devontae was fed up with the whole ordeal and decided to confront Nawiri about the situation. After class, he waited in the hallway by the door, listening for her distinctive Alto voice. 'Hey, Nawiri, can I talk to you for a second?' As soon a turned her head, he proceeded to ask, 'Why you always trynna steal my shine shorty? Math is my thing, I hear you good at everything, why can't you just let this one go?' he asked earnestly.

'Cause that's not how I roll Lil' Homie,' Nawiri replied. She turned away quickly and walked swiftly down the hallway laughing with Sasha.

'These girls are a trip!' thought Devontae, 'unreasonable ass!' He walked in the opposite direction, angry and disheartened. It was self-centered behavior like this that made him resent the school and want to transfer back to his neighborhood school. The only thing keeping him at Century was the promise of a brighter future and a ticket out of the hood; making friends was nowhere on his list of priorities.

The days were becoming shorter and the red, orange, deep purple and brown leaves had begun to make their way to the ground. On Nawiri's street, kids raked together huge piles of leaves and jumped in them joyfully. Their parents looked upon the madness through their windows, too conserved to face the brisk Fall wind. Nawiri loved Fall for the festivities. There were pumpkin patches, hay rides, pumpkin carving, haunted houses, apple orchards, soccer practice and soccer games, bike riding, even sitting on the porch and listening to the cars ride by bumping Biggie and DMX. Night time walks with her Grandmother, G'Ma, were her favorite – mosquitoes were retreating into their winter safe havens or dying, either way, everyone was glad they weren't around to sting their arms and legs.

One evening during one of their night time walks, Nawiri asked her grandmother, ''G'Ma, I've been thinking – I want to be an astronaut when I grow up. Do you think that is a realistic dream?'

'Of course it is sweetheart; I think it's a great idea! I would be so proud if you became an astronaut, actually I'll be proud no matter what you do baby. Why would you think that it's not realistic?' her Grandmother asked, concerned.

'Well, I don't know – because I'm black, I guess.' Nawiri replied. This was a statement that Ms. Heath had been dreading; she had worked so hard to protect and shelter her granddaughter when she was a little girl. Ms. Heath quietly and frantically tried to think of the best response, some combination of words that would curb her grandbaby's worries without acknowledging the gravity and depth of the question asked. 'Is it the t.v.?' She thought. 'Or maybe somebody said something to my baby. Don't let them come around me, I'll knock a nay-sayer into next week! We didn't fight for our rights all those years just for our babies to still be doubting themselves for the beautiful, brown color that God blessed them with.'

'That's ridiculous, look at May C. Jemison, she's black, she's a woman and she's an astronaut. And a trained doctor too. If our people could build pyramids, survive in deserts and rainforests, travel to the Americas long before that Christopher Columbus, pass down thousands of years of spoken word history, create written languages and peaceful Empires of gold, heal each other with nature's medicines, form the underground railroad, invent technologies that changed the world for the better, then there ain't nothin' you can't accomplish if you work hard baby, case closed!' G'Ma said definitively. 'Know thy self, baby girl, know thy self. I guess I need to pull out some history books for you to read, poor child don't know about her own righteous people.'

Nawiri looked up at her grandmother, entranced by her ever-present wisdom. To adopt such a confident approach to life seemed unreachable. Doubt began to creep into her thoughts as she wondered if Mae C. Jemison was the only black female astronaut her grandmother could name. Tempted to continue drilling her with questions, she decided to keep quiet, enjoy the walk and put her fears and doubts aside for another day. But the doubt was like a tiny seed growing in her mind. If she decided to water and cultivate it, then it could grow large enough to truly prevent her from accomplishing her dreams.

For many students, self-doubt had begun to affect their sense of confidence and hope. Nawiri could see and was afraid that it would take control of her in the same way. Feelings of inferiority manifested themselves into idleness and deep rooted anger. Like the ocean's high tides and low banks, mental resilience was extremely difficult amidst the emotional tsunamis of the young, impressionable mind – or so it seemed.

They walked on, changing the topic to Halloween costumes. Nawiri was determined to convince her grandmother that dressing up as a television set was the best option and that they needed to go purchase some spare TV parts to make the costume. G'Ma wasn't convinced; she didn't want to spend so much time and energy on a Halloween costume but Nawiri was being very persistent, especially since Sasha had already begun to work on her remote control costume. She didn't want Nawiri to be out on Halloween night but it was one of those sacrifices that parents and guardians made to make their children happy.

Nawiri walked into school on November first, the day after Halloween, tired and sore from her long night of trick-or-treating. It was a fun tradition even though her G'Ma didn't let her eat the candy because of some crazy diseases called diabetes and cavities.

While Nawiri was enjoying her night of sugary bliss, not all of her classmates could say the same. Even on this dark, chilly night, where happy, sugar-rushed children made their way swiftly though the streets, there was still danger lurking, ready to pounce and attack the guilty and the innocent.

LOST IN THE WORLD

Devontae lay on his bed, dreaming up a hole, a dark hole, the darkest he'd ever seen. It engulfed his entire body and he could feel the immense gravity pulling, twisting and contorting his frame. He had been reading so much about deep space and black holes that the images began to manifest themselves in his dreams. He travelled to galaxies, backward in time and forward in time, visited barren planets and overpopulated ones. The aliens he encountered were so friendly. Like the Native Americans, they accepted him as a brother. His landing was smooth, as the alignment of the stars had informed them that they should be expecting a visitor. Prepared for anything, they equipped themselves with armor and weapons for protection and collected food and water in case he was a peaceful visitor.

He opened his mouth to speak and they silenced him with weapons aimed at his heart. Through dark forest, rivers, streams and open plains, he followed his capturers as they led him to their village. This land was different in every way, the leaves of the trees were turquoise, the soil was orange like he'd never seen and the sky was so black, it was the first time he could see stars shine so brilliantly across a landscape. The inhabitants of these lands were like ghosts, appearing and disappearing as they weaved in and out of the trees. It was magical.

When they arrived, the village was invisible, only when the entrance was open could he see a lively race of beings moving to and fro, preparing meals, washing items. The small ones played and the mothers watched over them silently as they performed their chores, similar to the interactions of the human species. Their small, yet technologically advanced huts were the most surprising difference of all. Their lives seemed simple yet their homes were lit with UV lighting, shape shifting furniture, communal induction stovetops, solar-powered electronics, and a host of other green technologies that allowed them to survive in this invisible space, not altering the beautiful terrain outside of their isolated community of light, amidst the dark outdoors.

They led him to their chief who was adorned in loose black garbs. When the chief removed his hood, he could see that it was none other than his own father. He spoke to Devontae through his mind, telling him he was safe and that they would take care of him for as long as he needed shelter. He could see that his son was lost, in need of nurturing and guidance. They set him up in a room, his own tech hut. Like a cell, it was a circular community. There was an energy source in the middle of the unit, communal kitchen, recycling and waste center, playspaces and think tanks. It was a place where any dream was possible to bring to life.

Disturbed by a slight noise, he awoke from his light sleep in the compound of the unknown planet only to find a small alien, child staring at him; she smiled and told him not to be afraid of the coming rains that eventually even the puddles drowning him would dry. He was confused by her words and drifted back into his sleep.

His dad took him along with a group of hunters as they travelled through vast jungles of turquoise leaves. Carefully, he showed him how to use a bow and arrow. It was bonding time that they had never spent on Earth. He celebrated with them during their solstice festival and mourned with them during times of death.

When it came time for him to continue his journey throughout the universe, they supplied him with all of the rations, clothing and oxygen that he would need for approximately twenty thousand light years, enough for him to make it to Earth. They also supplied him with weapons, for this planet they had heard was full of chaos and angry inhabitants, who showed less hospitality to aliens and foreigners. He waved goodbye to his father and new found friends. Sad to leave this home away from home, he launched into space but his packages were too heavy for the gravity dense region and the turbulence shook him off course. Suddenly, he crash landed on a star, 'BOOM!!!!'

Within the explosion, the sound of shattering glass from his space ship pierced his ears as he awoke to the most excruciating pain. Bleeding from the inside out; the throbbing seemed to be coming from everywhere at the same time. He yelled out to his sister and rolled off of the bed, dragging himself to the door. Glass lay scattered around the bed from the stray bullets that had forced their way into his home and into his body, bringing him back from a loving dad, galaxies, stars and unknown planets to a place of drive-bys, bleeding wounds and vengeful niggas on the block.

THE SHOW GOES ON

The next day, Nawiri was greeted by Sasha with a grim message, 'Did you hear about what happened last night?'

'No, I just got here. What happened?' Nawiri asked, afraid to hear the answer.

'Devontae got shot! Once in the back and once in the leg, they say he's in critical condition. I think that means bad.'

Nawiri stood in shock, she had despised him as a math competitor but she would have never wished something like this even on her worst enemy. She tried to imagine how it must have felt for a small metal object to pierce her skin and organs. The shock of blood rushing, uncontrollably. And the horror of facing death before dreams of being an astronaut came true. She thought of how scared he must be and suddenly felt the urge to be at the hospital with him, by his side.

'Well, do you know exactly what happened or what? I need more information!' Nawiri asked, frantically.

'They said it was stray bullets from a drive by next door to him, apparently his next door neighbors are a part of a gang in his neighborhood,' Sasha replied, wiping her eyes and pulling herself together.

Nawiri felt responsible. Even though she had nothing to do with the situation, she thought perhaps her ill will towards him had affected his *chi*[1]. Worry escalated as recurring questions continued to cloud her mind. 'Is he going to survive? How is he going to do his homework while he's in the hospital? Who is attending to him? What if they don't know what they're doing? Why do we keep killing each other? Did their parents not teach them better? Is it the music? I bet it's the music. I wonder if he's awake right now. What is he thinking about? If I had've invited him to go trick-or-treating, he woulda been out with us. Oh my God, what have I done?'

Nawiri sat paralyzed through each of her classes. For someone she didn't know, it was strange that she felt she was losing one of her closest friends – he was an ally in the world of students conquering academic challenges in the face of adversity. And she didn't want to lose him.

After a month of being absent, Devontae returned to school. He used wooden crutches to assist him as he walked, adorned with an off white cushion embedded in the fold of the wood for armpit support. But he looked miserable. No amount of cushion or consolation seemed to make him smile. He kept his head tilted downward and his eyes cast to the ground as he hobbled through the hallways. In class, he no

---

[1] A term from Eastern Philosophies used to describe an individual's energy or life-force surrounding them.

longer sat astute waiting for the next question, instead he just stared out of the window as if he was lost in a daydream, his mind wandering aimlessly with heavy thought drowning him in anguish.

Life in the projects had never been easy. Devontae with his three siblings and single mother lived a modest life. They purchased what was necessary and prayed for the luxuries they desired. For Devontae, it was this humbling experience that inspired him to go to school every morning and prove to the world that his existence amounted to more than babysitting and chillin' on the corner on nights when the lights were off.

'He looks so sad,' Sasha said to Nawiri while placing her lunch box on the cafeteria table. She was watching him as he inched along the lunch food line. Nawiri turned, 'Yeah, I mean I would be sad too if I had to walk around with those crutches, it's uncomfortable.'

'I know but he should be happy that he's alive instead of moping around, feeling sorry for himself.' Sasha replied.

Nawiri turned back to her friend, surprised by her annoyance, 'Well, that's easy to say but none of us can tell him how he should feel because we have never been shot before. We don't know how much pain he's in and we don't know how angry he must be feeling right now.'

'That's true,' Sasha responded, regretful for passing judgment on her injured classmate.

After Algebra, Nawiri overheard Mr. Edison addressing some concerns with Devontae's recent performance. She walked slowly toward the door to catch as many words as possible, 'Is there a reason why you haven't been doing your homework? Because…Hold on, can I help you Ms. Simmons?' he looked up at Nawiri.

'No, I was just leaving Mr. Edison,' she hurried out of the door and into the hallway. 'I can't believe he hasn't been doing his homework!' she thought, 'How could he not care! He can't put his future on hold, he needs to keep going. The world isn't going to stop turning to wait for him to heal! Who does he think he is? I know he's hurt and all but what is he gonna do if he drops out of school? He would never be happy running the streets for the rest of his life. I've got to do something!'

Nawiri marched home determined to start her homework early to giver herself time to double check it and then do a second assignment to turn in as Devontae's. She decided that she would complete his homework assignments until he regained his motivation to complete them himself. 'At least if he passes math, they might pass him into the next grade and by then he'll be back to normal,' she thought.

Nawiri stayed up late into the night perfecting her new Devontae-inspired and imitated handwriting style. She had seen him write on the board and attempted to curve her letters, numbers and signs the way he curved his. He had that typical, sloppy boy handwriting, so she struggled at first but got the hang of it after a while. To create a more uneasy hand, she held the pencil between her middle and ring fingers instead of her middle and index finger. The hours slipped by and she found herself asleep at her desk at four o'clock in the morning. Waking up to the sounds of chirping birds, she finished his last two problems and headed to bed for a few extra hours of sleep.

For weeks, Nawiri continued this routine of completing one homework assignment for herself and one for Devontae. She wasn't sure how long she would be willing to keep this up because it was beginning to take a toll on her sleep schedule. G'Ma was even noticing and commenting on her sluggish behavior in the mornings and the pronounced bags under her eyes. As much as she wanted to be brave, Nawiri was afraid of getting in trouble and needed Devontae to cheer up before the next marking period.

'Ok class, today we are going to partake in a little surprise activity, please put away your notes and keep your pencil and calculator on top of your desk.' Mr. Edison exclaimed, preparing the class for a pop quiz. Nawiri and Sasha glanced at one another, confused. 'This pop quiz will consist of three questions, each taken directly from your last three homework assignments, so if you have been completing them and consistently scoring well, then you should have no problems,' he told the class.

Mr. Edison wrote the three problems on the board and headed to his desk to watch the students whither in annoyance at his 'little surprise.'

Nawiri left algebra confident that she had aced the quiz but she was worried that Devontae did not do well because he had not been completing the homework assignments himself. He, on the other hand, seemed to be just as indifferent about the quiz as he was about the homework. Some days he didn't even come to school; there were rumors that he had joined a gang to get revenge but no one really knew what was going through his mind. Besides his obvious apathy, he had also gained a large following of girls who thought it was somehow attractive to get shot and to endure a life threatening experience. Because of the girl magnet status, many of the guys also wanted to befriend him. Nawiri was starting to feel that maybe her help was in vain, he couldn't even be thankful for it because he didn't know. And besides, she didn't want to be just another groupie.

After school, Mr. Edison motioned for Nawiri to step into his classroom. There, she saw Devontae slouching in his seat with a grim facial expression. He let out a heavy sigh as she walked through the door, 'not this bitch again,' he thought. 'Have a seat Miss Simmons,' said Mr. Edison. He allowed her to settle into a desk before he began his interrogation. 'So, for the past few weeks I have been extremely proud of you, Mr. Harris for completing your homework assignments and handing them in on time. By your recently inexpressive behavior, I had assumed that you would not do the work but I was glad that you decided to continue to participate through homework even if you are no longer volunteering and answering questions in class like you did before. But I thought it was quite strange that you got every question wrong on today's quiz considering the fact that you have been doing so well on the homework. So, what does this have to do with Miss Simmons? Well, I took it upon myself to compare your handwriting to that of Devontae's recent homework and I can see that although you have tried to conceal your writing style, there are still some resemblances. Furthermore, these recent homework assignments are not written anything like those of Devontae's previous assignments. So my question to both of you is – was this a coordinated scheme and if so, why did you feel the need to be dishonest?' asked Mr. Edison, frankly.

'Man, I didn't even know she was doing my homework! I didn't ask her to do it, why you in my business, damn?' Devontae replied, turning angrily toward Nawiri.

Nawiri was shocked, holding her open palm to her chest as if she'd been stabbed with a verbal dagger. 'How can he be so ungrateful?' she thought.

Mr. Edison and Devontae turned toward Nawiri, looking upon her with inquisitive, harsh eyes. She felt like the room was spinning, her heart beat was racing and her hands were trembling as she placed them under the desk to hide her escalating anxiety. Mr. Edison began to pity her but held his stern face.

'I…I…I…just wanted to help!' she cried out, large salty tear drops clouding her eyes and fogging her glasses. She took them off and hastily wiped them with her shirt, keeping her eyes closed, to avoid the embarrassment.

'Miss Simmons, you do know this type of behavior is called cheating and it will not be tolerated in my classroom! And Mr. Harris, while I know you must be experiencing some post-traumatic stress, if you are going to be a student in this class, then my expectations of you will be on par with that of the rest of the class. If you ever need to talk, I'm here for you man but for now, you each have after school detention for the rest of the week!' He concluded definitively and left them there to face their actions in silence.

Nawiri was devastated. She had never been in so much trouble before and Devontae was angry, he felt like he was being punished, yet again, for something he had nothing to do with. He began to beat on his desk in defiance, shaking his head from side to side, 'Now, what if I had never been shot. This girl would still be steady trynna take my spot. Now I'm detention, looking dumb as hell. Ready to leave, somebody ring the bell. Look at her crying like she lost her favorite Bear. She has no idea the type of pain I bare.'

Devontae was quite the poet, sometimes his thoughts flowed like rhymes and manifested into rhythmical accentuated poetry also known as RAP. He was called 'Nu'' by the other children in his neighborhood because his flow was so different from other kids they heard. Older cats liked to call him young money because they predicted that he would one day get rich off of his lyrical talents, little did they know, he wanted to be a philosopher or an astronaut.

They sat silently wallowing in their own self-pity but after a while it got old and Nawiri finally decided to speak to him. After months of competition and rivalry, she mustered the courage to speak to the boy who had managed to become the center of her worries. 'You can at least say thank you,' she said softly, her voice was still raspy from the crying.

'Thank you, for what?' replied Devontae. 'Thank you for making my life more miserable than it already is? Thank you for thinking that you are so much better than me that you can compete with me in class and then do my own homework for me, like I can't do it myself? Yeah, thanks a lot…for nothin'!'

He turned his desk around to face the wall. For the next two days of detention he sat like this, in silence, listening to the ticks and tocks of the clock on the wall and Nawiri's light breathing. She had become used to his insolence and decided to wait patiently until he was ready to talk to her and as she had anticipated, he finally broke.

'So, your name is Nawiri, what does it mean?' Devontae asked.

'It means healthy,' Nawiri replied casually.

Devontae chuckled, 'Why healthy? Why not beautiful?'

'I don't know, my Mom says she liked it because she thought it would lead me to a healthy life and healthy relationships and ultimately happiness,' Nawiri replied gently. She didn't want to send him into a frenzy or upset his seemingly jumpy nerves, so she resolved to answering his questions without sounding defensive.

'Oh ok, that makes sense. So, you live around here?' he asked.

'Yeah, do you?' Nawiri asked, not knowing where the conversation was heading.

‘Yeah, where?’ Devontae pried further.

‘In Palmer Woods, off Seven Mile Road,’ Nawiri was jaded by his persistence.

‘Yup, that’s what I thought, rich! Ya’ll rich kids always doin’ what you want when you want, not givin’ a shit about anybody but yourselves. You almost fooled me with those flooded pants!’ Devontae laughed.

‘What is your problem?!’ Nawiri stood up, ‘you think the world owes you somethin’ cause you got shot? Get over yourself! I was trynna help you and I’m sorry that I did it without talking to you first but you don’t have to go insulting me! I don’t think I deserve that! I feel for your situation, I really do but you know it could always be worse. You could have died but you’re still here. God gave you a second chance at life, you gotta take advantage of it like you were doing before.’ Nawiri sat down, panting. She felt as if she had just completed a theatrical performance and she hoped it was well received. ‘Why is he smiling? What a jerk!’ she thought.

‘Wow, that was cute,’ Devontae laughed. ‘Ok, ok, I’m sorry. I should be thankful for life and thankful for those who care enough to help me out in a time of need. Thank you for trying to help, maybe next time you can TALK to me first and see if I NEED it instead of just making assumptions. I was gonna do the homework eventually but I’m glad to know I got a lil’shawty lookin’ out.’

‘Well, I don’t know about all this lil’shawty stuff but you’re welcome,’ Nawiri smiled, relieved that he didn’t yell back at her. Although he looked rough and mean on the outside, his laugh and kind words showed her that there was still a light shining in him that no person or bullet could take away.

GOLDEN

The next day, the lunch room was crowded, as usual. Nawiri and Sasha picked a table and sat down with their bagged lunches. Sasha was the first to pull out the contents of her lunch box. She had a turkey sandwich with lettuce, tomato, and mustard on whole wheat bread, a bag of chips, an apple and a water bottle. Nawiri took out her Caesar salad ingredients and started to combine the lettuce, beets, black olives, grilled chicken strips and Caesar dressing. She also had a piece of whole grain bread and a bottle of 100% orange juice. Nawiri's grandmother was adamant about eating healthy and Sasha, who packed her own lunches, copied Nawiri's lunches as best she could. They had grown to prefer these healthy choices over the junk food in the vending machines and the greasy hot lunches that they served in school.

Nawiri looked up from her salad assembly and caught eyes with Devontae as he searched for a lunch table where he would feel decently comfortable without having to engage in much useless conversation. She motioned for him to join them and he made his way over, reluctantly.

‘Hey you,’ Nawiri and Sasha chorused together. ‘Hey,’ Devontae replied. ‘I like those shoes!’ Nawiri complimented Devontae, ‘where you get them from? They Air Force 1’s right? But who put all those designs on the side?’

‘I bought the plain white low tops from the mall when they went on sale and then my boy on the block spray painted them for me.’

‘So, let’s say I get a white pair, can your boy paint mine too?’ Nawiri smiled, raising her eyebrows in anticipation. She wasn’t really that into gym shoes but wanted to find a talking point quickly before the introduction of the deafening silence that accompanied kids thinking of things to say to one another and finding nothing. It would have been irrelevant for her to wait until he sat down when the shoes were under the table, so she jumped on the opportunity to create a conversation before it slipped away.

‘I guess, just let me know what design you want and he can hook you up. It might cost you around twenty dollars.’

‘Ok, great! So, anyway, what is that on your tray?’

‘It’s chicken strips and fries. Why? You want some?’ Devontae asked.

They all stared down at the glistening chicken on his tray. Nawiri couldn’t decide if her mouth was watering because of the appetizing smell or because of the dripping grease that was making her gag. The golden chicken had come all the way from a factory in Ohio, where they were bred in the thousands (some even say cloned), fed corn meal, pumped with steroids and anti-biotics, plucked, shucked, boiled, diced, ground, layered in glue, powdered with flour and frozen. Delivered 'fresh' to Century Academy for frying and consumption.

'Oh, no thank you. All that brown, I was just wondering what was what. I don't understand why they can't serve more colorful food. They got broccoli up there, why didn't you get some?'

'That stuff is all mush, soon as you put it in your mouth it just slides down your throat. I wanna chew my vegetables.'

They all laughed.

Devontae began to devour the chicken, looking up as often as possible to show Nawiri and Sasha just how much he was enjoying his fried, brown food. He looked pleased enough to be an official representative for the cafeteria kitchen. Although the kitchen often sold itself – fast service, a shiny tray table, steaming hot food – not to mention the lack of alternative options. In fact, the majority of the children around them purchased the school lunch every day. Unbeknownst to Sasha and Nawiri, Devontae was also a part of the reduced cost lunch program. So, this was his cheapest option and essentially his only option.

Lunch periods from that day forward changed from a duo to a trio. They were surprisingly enjoying one another's company. One boy and two girls. Devontae sometimes felt he needed a male counterpart to even out the hormone imbalance but this combination was satisfactory for the time being. Plus, the three were inseparable at lunch, mostly because Devontae told constant jokes, Nawiri's sarcasm prompted him to continue and Sasha was always an amused member of their front row audience. Her laugh fueled the excitement. Many times they were so loud that they drew interest from those around them and by the end of the lunch period, the entire table was either participating or listening to Devontae and Nawiri going back and forth about one another's clothing and they especially loved to make fun of the other person's food.

'Look at that lettuce! Are those brown spots healthy? I think that means you got pesticides on your lettuce. You still gon' eat that? I thought you were healthy. No?'

'This is organic thank you very much! Maybe I should just go grab a hamburger, so I can smear grease and ketchup all over my face like you!'

Sasha laughed and Devontae quickly reached for a napkin, while Nawiri held them away from him, so that he scrambled to get a hold of the napkin box, tripped and landed on the floor.

This was the typical, lively scene; a battle between a lover of apples and a lover of fries.

One day, Devontae forgot money for lunch and Nawiri split her tuna salad sandwich with him. He was surprisingly pleased with the taste and while he made jokes about the sandwich, he asked her to bring him another one. This was the start of Nawiri's healthy lunch food victories.

DAYDREAMIN

I'm flying high in the sky,

Feeling like a feather or a firefly.

My balance is undefined,

The wind carries me.

My nerves are unending

Or maybe just on edge.

My senses are stunned.

I can't see,

I can't hear,

My body is free.

My mind is clear.

It is emptiness.

Soon,

I'll be on my way.

Sasha Gordon wrote poetry. The form and sensuality of a poem was an expression that linked her mind, body, spirit, *and* soul. She was a dreamer, a fanatic of sorts. Lost in her private thoughts; she dreamed of success, gratification, and bigger possibilities in a bigger world with better people and better things. With her grandiose visions, she also had a dark sense of reality, often carrying the heaviness of the world on her shoulders. Happiness could quickly yield to somber thoughts of death and pain with a glance at a picture, a whiff of some aroma or the sudden shouting from her mother. Even in the days of televisions, cell phones, computers, and sports cars – oppression, racism, corruption and injustice were still evident. These epidemics were broadcast on the daily news, they breathed fire around the street corners; they existed within establishments, in foreign countries and even within the nation's capital. In these moments of awareness, Sasha would feel a jolting rush of anger and an impulse to change such chaotic and destructive tides. Perhaps it was a deflection from her own chaotic mind.

In her efforts of self-comfort for her personal struggles and for the peoples of the world, she found pleasure and peace in writing poetry. Her poetry was many times universal and she felt as if the words possessed a power that was unattainable through her physical self.

There was a growing anticipation in her heart to thrive but a nagging sense of doubt as to how to actually accomplish her goals. She worked during the day to be a pillar of strength and often fell, at night, back into worry and internal scrutiny. She would sometimes write, sometimes run away, sometimes wrap up in a blanket and try to rock the worries, the pain, and the secrets away. Her poem today, like many others, had no definite ending. This, she knew, represented her uncertainties about life.

Her eyes burst open, early in the morning, to the sound of a monstrous voice. Her fingers gripped the sheets as her heartbeat slowed back down to normal pace. Ears ringing, she slid angrily out of bed.

'Sasha!!!!' her mother hollered. 'Come get these damn clothes outta the dryer! How many times do I got to ask your non-hearin', lazy ass?'

'I'm sorry mama, I just woke up.' Sasha stammered as she pulled on pants and socks hurriedly.

'Sorry my ass. And why is there a dish still sitting in my sink? You make me so sick. Before you even get the notion, I'm telling you now, you can't do nothin' tonight.'

'But why, mama? I did everything you asked. That dish is from the snack YOU ate at like twelve o'clock last night and I just put those clothes in the dryer!'

'That don't make a damn bit o' difference, just get yo' ass downstairs and do what I told you to do before I hurt you! Plus, you gotta baby-sit your sister tonight anyway!'

As Sasha sulked down the stairs, she thought, 'No matter what I do, it's never good enough. Why God, did you curse me with a mother like this. What did I do to deserve a mad woman for my momma?'

She washed the dishes slowly, letting the hot water scold her hand while concentrating on somber thoughts. An ant scurried across the countertop. 'Damn ants!' there was nothing worse than spotting an ant on a Sunday. The ultimate disrespect to the household and to her already compromised emotional state. The bugs seemed to be appearing from thin air, first the ant, then a gnat that buzzed and flipped and twirled, fluttering conveniently around the garbage disposal and thus around Sasha, who stood at the sinking ducking and dodging instead of just lifting her hand out of the foamy water to swat him away. There was enough stimulation at the kitchen sink to keep her busy all day. Finding gnat dodging to be useless, she began to ignore him and stared out of her window at the handsome boys playing basketball at the park across the street. Well, maybe not handsome but it was obvious that they had at least been doing their sit ups at night and their push-ups in the morning. Her mind jumped ahead to the future where she saw herself standing in her own apartment, living by her own rules and walking down the street with one of the fine, shirtless boys that were holding her attention so well.

Some people thought she was crazy the way she dared to walk down the street with her head held high, not giving any satisfaction to the gawkers or the haters. No eye contact, no waves, no hellos, just sheer indifference. Her mind was so entrenched in thoughts that many of her peers misperceived her aloof nature as arrogance. Sasha was completely oblivious, engrossed in serious thoughts about the many events in her life, some making her smile and others bringing tears to her eyes. Self-confidence was a trait, a natural gift that most had assigned to her but something that she - herself - could not feel. She was just being, living, loving, experimenting, and trying to fit into social norms the best way she could.

In quiet moments alone, every emotion was set loose in an external rampage. First, it would be a laugh, perhaps at something that occurred earlier in the day, then an exhausted huff, followed by an outburst of tears. The laughter was bitter and the tears were sweet with a sour after taste like lemon drops. Incarcerated thoughts made their way into journals whose pages were stained by her lemon tears. Her mother's wrath had thickened her skin and dulled an otherwise lively spirit. Those convoluted feelings, reactions to the wrath, found their way into the journals. It was an eclectic mix with the rest of her thoughts about the world.

Sasha, her mother - Ms. Karena, and her little sister, Niamako, lived in a small bungalow on the East Side of Detroit. Her older brother had joined the military and her father was somewhere, she didn't know where and had grown not to care. He and Ms. Karena divorced after a dreadful five years. And Sasha had been forced to accept that her father was a rolling stone and many other horrible things according to her mother, like a monster and a control freak but she was skeptical as she had never heard his side of the story and didn't remember much about him.

Ms. Karena reclined in her lawn chair and lit a cigarette, the evening air was cool. She could feel Fall giving way to Winter but wasn't ready to stop her evenings on the front porch, relaxing with a scotch in one hand and a cigarette in the other. She had come a long way from the gutter, worked hard to pay the bills and never missed an opportunity to remind her kids of the sacrifices she had made for them. In her twenties, she had been so beautiful; all the brothers were trying to holla. It was a beauty that she had so generously passed down to her daughters. She waitressed, escorted, did nails, worked in high fashion clothing stores and always wore the latest fashions. She was the envy of her peers. But what she loved to do the most, was sing. A natural born singer, Ms. Karena sung in the church, at home, in the evening, in the morning, in the club, on the street, anytime there was an ear to listen, she sang because she wanted the whole world to know that she had talent. And just when the hype started to build, the talent scouts started calling and the record labels were ready to have her sign by the X, she met L.J. Gordon, the finest man to ever cross her path.

He had charm, boy did he have charm. The kind that would make any woman, without a strong backbone, melt right into the floor if she wasn't already there just by the looks of him. Tall, milk-chocolate man, with almond eyes and a firm, square jaw. His gaze was electrifying. Ms. Karena knew, even before he spoke, that he would be the father of her unborn children and a step father to her six year old son. Within the first ten minutes of their conversation, as she assisted him throughout the clothing store, she had already conjured up a perfect, harmonious life for the two of them. A life where their kids had a functional, beautiful family unlike hers where there were nine kids and only a drunken father to look after them.

Apparently, he had been drawn to her beauty as well, for they had no trouble exchanging numbers and starting a relationship that would change her life forever.

His full name was Lincoln James Gordon, L.J. for short. He was ten years Ms. Karena's senior but no one – not even his own mother – could tell. Delving into the relationship like two kids into a Godiva Chocolate box, their love grew exponentially, taking them each by surprise. Long walks along the riverfront, shopping trips to New York City, road trips to Georgia, wine tastings, and adventurous, intoxicating sex. It was as sweet as the first drops of mango juice that send the tongue into a state of blissful awakening. Their connection was like a constant adrenaline rush; exhilarating, intimidating perfection. Which is probably why it eventually spiraled out of control.

The first time he hit her, she convinced herself that it hadn't really happened, attributed the bruise to the fall and the shock – to love's adrenaline rush. The second time, she knew it was real. L.J. had come home drunk, of course, accusing her of sleeping around. She wasn't afraid because she knew the first time was only her imagination, so there could be no second if there was no first. All she could remember from before the blackness was the purple lamp shade that her sister had bought for her twentieth birthday, the retro tassels were swinging wildly – then blackness. The following hospital experience was too real, back and forth from the trauma burn unit to the Psychologist to anyone else employed in the hospital system who thought it was their business to make the situation feel more tangible than the imaginary one she was trying to make it into, like the first time. It was useless; her scalp healed and she was back with him, accepting his grave apologies, loving the warmth of his kisses and reminiscing about the days of long walks and cross-country excursions. It was only a matter of time before she had two young children, a two bedroom bungalow and a husband, who continued to verbally and physically abuse.

In disbelief that she had allowed her life to become a mirror image of the environment she had grown up in, she was too ashamed to open up to her brothers and sisters about her situation. 'Most of them got their own drama to deal with anyway,' she thought, 'Why would I worry them with my problems? At least I'm still sober and sane, unlike Janice and Natalie. Still alive, unlike poor Robbie. God Bless his soul. Still beautiful, unlike Shelby and Donald. And still thin, unlike Clarence, Larry and Marvina. Daddy would sure be proud of us! Humph, Momma's probably rolling in her grave right now. Well, she probably been rolling for a long time. I wonder would she have been strong enough to control Daddy's temper. Why don't I have that type of strength? What do I have to change to make him stop? Maybe if I make dinner earlier, I'll have time to buff his shoes. Or I can give him a back rub every other day, to ease some of that stress and tension out of his body. Lord, what a woman will do to keep a man happy. And yet they still don't seem to give a damn. If I just ended it all right now, somebody would take care of my kids, probably better than I can, and he would never be able to put his hands on my living, breathing body again.'

On top of the abuse, she hated that he didn't support her music career. She was forced to stop her singing and working in order to stay home and look after the children. Her life had become like an episode of her most despised television show where she hated the characters, including herself and felt she had no control over what was happening.

Until one day, Ms. Karena Gordon had had enough. He stumbled into the house, breath harsh and toxic with words and chemical smells spewing out. The children ran to Ms. Karena as she stared at him with pity in her eyes. Wondering how life could bring such a beautiful black man to such a low place. Backing into a corner with the girls hovering near her knees, she covered her head, preparing for the ensuing blows. The floor shook as he stormed forward, picture frames falling in his path as if an earthquake was upon them. Removing the foundation from beneath their feet. She stood still and hunched peaking underneath her forearm. She swore it was God and only God that stepped between his hands and her neck that day. As he approached swiftly, the television cord sneaked up from beneath the vintage green rug she had purchased at the thrift store on a whim. His arms went flailing in the air as he fell to the ground with a huge thump. They peered down at him, the man who was supposed to be their protector, as he lay unconscious from the impact. She stepped over his body carefully and ran to the phone. Called the police – teeth chattering and from head to toe her body shook with fear. She stared at the floor, anticipating his sudden awakening but this time, everything went according to plan. She had enough evidence to put him away for a long time. She filed for divorce, moved to another neighborhood in the city and never took the kids to visit him in jail once. Her voice, by that time, was ruined, so she settled for a steady paying, minimum wage job to cover the bills and tried to focus on raising her children the 'right' way.

Ms. Karena went on to get a degree in managerial studies and landed a job in the human resources department of a real-estate firm. The work wasn't too demanding and the pay was decent; enough to put food on the table, pay bills and provide a constant supply of money for her frequent trips to strip malls, outlets, boutiques and mega centers. This was before the online shopping boom, before debit cards and Macy's emails. So, she searched newspapers and magazines for sales and coupons. Took her Toyota Camry right down the street to Eastland Mall and if she was really feeling fancy, Somerset Mall or adventurous, the Outlet Mall in Traverse City. Anything new got her mind off of the past and glued to the present.

She walked into work fresh to death with pencil skirts, flowing blouses and heels of all shapes and sizes to match. Everyone in the office admired her style and Detroit swag. She even caught her boss, a white man from South Dakota, sizing her up from time to time but paid little attention to him unless he was giving assignments or correcting her work.

One snowy day, when many employees had called off of work, he attempted to instruct her to do more than what her job description required. He called her to his office toward the end of the work day and asked her how she was feeling. She assured him that she was feeling well and satisfied in her position. Then he proceeded to ask more personal questions about her life, her children and husband. Feeling uncomfortable, she stood up to leave and saw that he was masturbating as they were talking.

As she ran to the door to get away, he locked it from his desk. 'Why don't you just come on over here and give me a blow job before you go, I'll give you a promotion tomorrow and you'll never have to work over time again for as long as you work here.' Ms. Karena could feel the hot, angry tears streaming down her face, 'You dirty bastard, if you don't let me out of this office in five seconds, I will cut your lifeless heart out of your chest myself and ship it to your wife and children for Thanksgiving.' Disappointed, he unlocked the door and she ran directly to the Human Resources office. She filed a grievance with the company, settled a lawsuit for a quarter million dollars and quit the job before they could beg her to stay.

Life was easy for those few years. No work, just relaxation, island and cruise vacations with summer romances. Bought the kids every doll, playhouse, stuffed animal, and designer clothing item you could think of. Two cars and an addition on the back of the house. Upgraded television sets in every room, every year. Thought about buying a boat but decided it would take up too much room in the backyard, plus the neighbors might start wondering what else she had in the house. Just when she was about to remodel the kitchen and refurnish the living room, the money ran out. She couldn't bring herself to face her own irresponsible spending, so she blamed the lost money on the kids for soaking up it all up on toys. 'These damn kids are just too damn spoiled, that's the problem! They done taken my last dime, I wish I could just give them away sometimes!' With no cash flow, she took a secretarial position at the local community college where she spent most of her time faxing papers, mailing letters, and gossiping about the latest office drama on smoke breaks.

They lived in an area called Conner Creek between Mack and Gratiot Avenue. The air was heavy from the fumes emitted by the local incinerator. Abandoned manufacturing sites housed barrels filled with leftover chemicals and waste and the industrial buildings were prime locations for illegal activities. The old railroad tracks served as play territory for young children and contributed to the distinct character of the neighborhood. The kids were fierce, hard as rocks, asthma plagued their small, developing lungs but they ran anyway. Chasing their rivals and running away from them. Dancing to hip hop at backyard parties and playing games – like tag and dodge ball at the park, daring any asthma attack to ruin their day.

This working class neighborhood had certainly transformed over the years. Although the vast majority of the homes were still inhabited, the number of unoccupied homes was slowly growing and like many urban 'hoods' the sense of community had diminished since the 70's. Once upon a time, neighbors would greet one another, know each other by first and last name, babysit, lend sugar, and so on. But times had changed and more and more it was just every man for himself.

One day, after school, Sasha noticed three of her rivals walking on the opposite side of the street, a short distance behind her. The recent snowfall had made the pavement slippery, so she twirled to get a better look. The three girls were known for being rough but concerning Sasha, for hating her. The girls were awkwardly mismatched, one was short with light skin and freckles; the second tall and meaty, with skin dark as the nighttime sky; and, the third was a medium height with brown skin, large eyes and a grimace to scare away even the most vicious of animals. With all of their stark physical differences, each shared one common feature and that was their weave ponytails.

Knowing that they lived right around the corner, Sasha had no choice but to fight them today. Otherwise, they would forever be hunting her down. This rivalry had existed since elementary school. When Sasha attended the neighborhood school, she was hated by so many of the girls because of the attention she received from boys, young and old. Her good grades didn't make the situation much better, in fact, they made it much worse. Jealousy heightened by the horror of being called white every time she scored well on a homework assignment or quiz. She had known more shapes, colors, words, animals, and tree types than anyone else in Kindergarten, with lovely handwriting to match her uncompromising smarts. This day was long overdue; it was she who had prolonged it. She had known this day would come, now it was time for her to prove that she was no longer the little girl who they used to bully and intimidate.

Sasha looked down at her hands, wondering if they would protect her. Wondering if her small fists were capable of doing anything beyond making solid snowballs and shaping cookie dough. Or if her arms were strong enough to deliver an impactful blow without falling out their sockets. Settling on agility as her weapon of defense, she did another twirl and found the girls on her side of the street, a few paces away. She stopped, carefully placed her book bag on the ground, and waited for them.

'I can't stand that bitch, Sasha, she think she is too cute.' They talked amongst themselves as if she was not in ear shot.

'Yeah, females like dat deserve ta get dey ass beat.'

'Yeah, Shanisha, I say you hit her in the mouth.'

'Oh, and what a coincidence, there she go right there waitin' for us.'

The girls walked up to Sasha casually and in the motion of a walking arm, Shanisha, balled up her fist and swung at Sasha's face. Though Sasha was small, her quickness caught the girls off guard, she ducked out of the way and before they could blink an eye, Shanisha fell to the ground, slipping on the pavement ice, and her bottom teeth had first impact, sending them straight through her mouth and onto the ground. The other girls stood watching, forgetting their loyalty. The blows did not stop there, they fell on the ground, rolling and sliding on the ice, scratching and kicking until they had no energy left and Sasha was the obvious winner. She grabbed her backpack quickly and ran for miles, it seemed, with her heavy Social Studies book pounding against her lower back. She ran with diligence at first, then with exhaustion, and finally she stalled in front of her house and fell asleep on the front porch, shivering, until she felt a slap on her aching back from Ms. Karena and a loud order to 'get your stupid ass up!'

OUT MY MIND, JUST IN TIME

'Ms. Heath, Ms. Heath!' called Mrs. Thompson from next door. 'Can you just take a quick look at my tomatoes, I think I might have an insect problem. You see these yellow spots here?'

'Yeah, it looks like your tomatoes might have some sorta fungal infection honey. You should go pick up some Red Mulch from the store, and lay it right down there, that should solve your problem Sherita. How's everything going by the way? How's Jerry and the kids?'

'Oh, you know. They're driving me crazy as usual but I love'em to death. Jerry just started a new job, so I've taken off a few months to help transition the kids into the new school year.'

'Oh yes, I know about that transition! Nawiri wanted all new accessories and gear, I told her she could get a new backpack, notebooks and pencils but I think the uniform still looks good.'

'I know that's right, these four boys here wear hand-me downs every year. I don't see a need to keep buying clothes that they'll outgrow in six months.'

‘I know that’s right honey. Well, I gotta run and do my morning meditation before it’s time to take Nawiri to school. I’ll talk to you later Sherita.’

They waved goodbye and Ms. Heath made her way back through the side door. The kitchen was beginning to brighten from the rising sun. The various crystal and glass ornaments on the window seal threw their sparkling reflections onto the walls, the floor and the kitchen table. The color scheme was mauve and light green which went well with the oak cabinets and beige tile floor.

Every room of the house, in fact, had a color scheme with decorative art that showed the sense of style and knack for interior design of Ms. Robyn, Nawiri’s mother. From the drapery to the choice of carpet, each room was fit for the most casual guest to the most distinctive.

The naked house without any decoration was like a beautiful unadorned landscape. Red brick, tutor-style, hard wood floors, seven bedrooms, and living quarters above the three car garage, which she used for a private, work studio.

The house had previously been home to a young family of three but the tall, dark picturesque figure of a man, had been more like a ghost, in an eerie state of existence, making his abrupt departure inevitable. Ms. Robyn tried to erase him from her memory, or at least the feelings that were so deeply rooted in her relationship with her ex-husband - the stealth, black tiger that he was. She couldn’t even remember his features, his laugh, or his interests. It was as if she had only imagined that she was married for ten years. His secrets and lies had created an atmosphere of complete confusion and frustration, making her doubt her own sensibilities. When she asked him where he was going, it was 'out.' When she asked him where he'd been, it was 'work.' When she asked if was he hungry, it was usually 'No.' Then, in the middle of the night, she could hear him making his way to the kitchen to prepare his own food. Red and orange stains on his shirt collar were from scratches, bleeding red pens and sweat from walking nine holes of golf. Foreign, fragrant smells were blamed on business clientele and fresh flowers in the office. Trips were frequent. Conversations – short and bitter. Smiles – forced. Hugs – one-armed. And kisses – quick and distasteful.

But what bothered her the most was his avoidance of Nawiri. It was as if he was afraid to interact with his own daughter. When she called out 'Daddy,' he would look the other way, go outside, or in some instances, leave the house completely. Nawiri looked after him as he left the house, her tiny forehead resting on the side door glass. She waited patiently, her feet cold from the winter air creeping in underneath the door frame, until her mother came to drag her away.

Ms. Robyn had loved his serious and pensive demeanor before they were married but dealing with it from day-to-day had become analogous to dying a slow death. The death of their family, their love, their communication and ultimately a miscarriage – the death of their unborn child. One day, in the midst of the anger and loneliness, she realized that she had chosen a life of despair and needed to change it. He existed as a shadow in her mind, clouding her memory and altering her judgment. She couldn't even recall his favorite color.

After their divorce, Mr. Simmons decided to move to California, or at least that's what he told them, and had made no effort to contact Ms. Robyn or his daughter, in six years.

After the miscarriage and the divorce, Ms. Robyn went into a 'zone.' Despite her efforts to appear happy, she packed her misery away into a deep, dark abyss. A treasure chest that she never planned to open again. The pain was stored there, yet so was the compassion. Her eyes became glazed as if she was no longer sharing the same reality with those around her. She invited her mother to live with she and Nawiri. 'Just for comforts sake,' she told them. 'No sense of having this huge house with only two people to fill it, let's invite grandma to stay with us!!' She said to the six year old Nawiri with enthusiasm. Ms. Heath, G'ma, moved in with no hesitation. She was happy to make a change from so many years of living in the South and Robyn was her only daughter and thus her favorite daughter. Ms. Heath new that her daughter was experiencing emotional trauma but was unsure how to approach her knowing that she had locked up her feelings in a private place. Patience was the option she chose. Yet, over the years it was becoming more and more clear that Ms. Robyn was no longer interested in being a mother and Ms. Heath had slowly taken her place in Nawiri's life.

Lying out her yoga mat, G'Ma began to do the stretches that her physical therapist had recommended to her. It had been over a year since she fractured her hip bone and she was determined to heal and become more flexible at the same time. Counting 1-2-3-4-5-6-7-8 and backwards until it was time to change the pose. The transformative power of stretching and meditation had saved her from sustaining more injuries and from drastic aging. This seventy five year old beauty looked not a day older than sixty. 'They say black don't crack and I'm living, breathing proof,' she would say to her quilting buddies, church sisters and close neighbors. Even Nawiri was learning her meditation techniques as a way to cope with school stress and to clear her mind of worries and obsessive competing. Although she continued to struggle with the latter.

After thirty minutes, Ms. Heath stood just in time for Nawiri to burst in with an exciting proposal. 'G'Ma! I have an idea, let me skip school today and we can go grocery shopping because I want to find some tofu for Devontae and then I'll make him some tofu, pesto sauce with noodles, using the parsley that we're growing in the backyard but since I don't know how to cook, I will need the whole day to prepare it. It's all about this competition we have going and of course I have to win because I just have to and…'

'Um, excuse me Miss Thang. But I'm not gonna let you to skip school to cook lunch for some little boy.' Ms. Heath laughed in disbelief. 'I'm not too busy today; maybe I'll take a few hours to prepare the dish with basil, not parsley, for your lunch tomorrow. And I don't understand why you keep taking this boy lunch. He ain't got no lunch of his own?'

'He does but if you saw it, you wouldn't want him to eat it either. The school lunch is always greasy and nasty-looking. So, if I have enough for two people, then I would rather share than to watch him eat that crap!' Nawiri proclaimed.

'Hmm, I see. Well, maybe I need to go on up there and have a talk with the food staff. There's got to be something we can do about providing some healthier food for you kids. But in the meantime, you need to worry about your own diet and school work. You can only skip school when you got the flu, the chicken pox, that horrible pneumonia or something so bad that we think you might die. And even then, I will lay that homework right on your bed!'

'Really?! Wow, G'Ma. That is no fair.'

'Life isn't fair child. Let's go or you'll be late. Fried egg sandwich and salsa for breakfast?'

'Yes, please! And can I have a yogurt too?' Nawiri replied excitedly.

Ms. Heath was a stickler for education. She had worked as a domestic all her life just so that her children could climb their way up the educational ladder. She couldn't give them much financial support but she gave all them all the love and encouragement they could ask for. In this same way, she was determined that her granddaughter take full advantage of her educational opportunities.

Mr. Heath had been a farmer, so she knew all about land. In Georgia, they had peach trees, orange trees, tomato vines, corn fields, collards, sweet potatoes, and yellow squash. She knew how to grow almost every plant imaginable. And she applied her knowledge of growing plants to raising children. They both required nurturing, a safe environment, water, food and loads of attention.

Ms. Robyn, on the other hand, felt Nawiri had no excuse for failure since she was financially stable and could afford to buy her daughter supplies and technological gadgets, send her to enrichment camps and pay for private tutors if necessary. Ms. Robyn would say to her friends, 'The wealth that I have accumulated should surely be enough to secure my daughter's future. I have no doubt that she will make the most of her resources.' But Ms. Heath had her doubts as she knew that love and attention were key ingredients that Nawiri was not receiving from her mother.

While she claimed to be down-to-earth, Ms. Robyn's bourgeoisie circles certainly contradicted this self-proclaimed identity, which Nawiri was never too shy to point out. 'Mom, you should adopt!' 'Mom, you ought to do more community service!' 'Why don't you talk to our family? Do they embarrass you? Why don't you talk to me? Do you still love me?'

Ms. Robyn would brush off such questions with blunt responses, 'There's not enough time in the day to take care of you and the whole world,' 'One must take care of themselves first before tending to everyone else's needs.' She would walk away rolling her eyes in annoyance. Pushing self-reflection into the dark, untouchable places in her mind.

Once upon a time, she had a vision to do such things as reach out to her others but she had become comfortable in her elite bubble and altered reality. Intimidated by the problems of the outside world, not willing to burst the bubble that so graciously sheltered her. Truthfully, people less fortunate than herself made her uncomfortable. She felt that they were ignorant, devoid of ambition and good work ethics. Scum of the earth, people with no hope of deliverance from suffering for their lack of education and motivation. Her closed heart went to show that even her mother and her daughter had been tuned out and could not influence her opinions. And her prejudices began to guide her actions such that her realm of understanding could only extend slightly into the human condition.

Ms. Heath was getting sick of her daughter's selfishness. And worried if she didn't find an intervention soon that Nawiri would grow to resent her mother and never forgive her. Arguing, however, would surely prove useless. So, the wait continued as she observed her daughter carefully, looking for the perfect moment to dive into the abyss and open the chest of secret feelings in Robyn's troubled mind.

ALL OF THE LIGHTS

Cambria opened up a snickers bar and starred out of the window. She was irritated but too entranced in her private thoughts to scold the obnoxious kids standing next to her, for disturbing the peace. The morning was chilly. October always brought beautiful colors and biting morning winds, the kind that kept Cambria's bones shaking and fueled her bitter contempt for the elderly bus driver, Mr. Brown, who never drove fast enough to catch any of the green lights. Riding through her neighborhood early in the morning, she always saw people she knew, doing things they shouldn't have been doing. Mr. Jones always put his extra trash in Ms. Rose's can without asking. Ms. Victoria, Niko and Cece's mother, was out destroying Ms. Rita's grass with her enormous SUV even though she always blamed it on her visitors. Rony's lover was sneaking out of the back window. Mr. Waters, a recovering alcoholic, was downing a bottle of scotch before his wife got up for work, discarding the empty bottle in Ms. Rose's trash, following in Mr. Jones' footsteps. Cambria thought how humorous it was that people were so cool, calm and collected in the evening, either sleep during the day or hard at work, but awkward and silly in the morning because they thought no one was paying attention. Living in the projects, she came to value the humanity that existed there even in the midst of violence, drugs, prostitution, roaming children, graffiti, gangs, and in littered alleyways paraded on the evening news. Of course, there were those who were irresponsible, never cut their grass, never tended to their gardens, and let their kids stay out in the streets until midnight, making too much noise, but most people were just trying to get by; to live another day to see their families, converse with neighbors and of course be woken by the brilliant morning sun. Momma used to wake up cheerful and energetic, when the sun came beaming through the windows of the house. Maybe she still did, but she was hardly ever there now, so Cambria had no idea what her mother's mood was like these days.

Momma Kiesha was usually high – eyes searching, mind wandering, body moving slowly about dark corridors, leaving the doors of the house open, where her children lie awake; scared of gloomy nighttime noises, creeks and moans. She could barely hear their fearful cries as she moved further and further away; her ears drowning in loud, distorted music. They watched cartoons day in and day out, during the summer months, and on the weekends, during the school year. Each cereal was paired to a specific movie. When they watched Peter Pan, they ate Captain Crunch!!! When they ate Lucky Charms, they watched the Snow White and the Seven Dwarfs!!!!! Everyone was on an ultimate high; momma had her white powder and the kids had their white, crystallized sugar.

The days slipped by; unaware of the time, stomachs full of Jolly Ranchers, Gummy Worms, Twizzlers, Sour Patch Kids, Make Me Happys, and Hide the Pains. They made it all go away, they made life fun – fun, fun, fun – everything had to be exciting otherwise they got bored and restless, no book was interesting enough or conversation exciting enough. They invented new games and watched new movies and played with new toys to avoid the agitation of boredom that would surely slow down their hyper-stimulated minds.

Devontae liked to be 'different' as his siblings saw him. He would shut himself away in his room or in any empty, semi-private corner, to read. He went to the public library and checked out three books every week, just to read on his spare time. When he wasn't reading, he was doing homework. And when he wasn't doing homework, he was writing rap lyrics or sleeping. Cambria let her brother be, she made sure to take him a plate of fried chicken and corn bread, spaghetti, a hamburger, or whatever else she decided to cook for dinner. Devontae didn't much like to talk to his older sister. They seemed to have very little in common. She liked to hang around outside and to play with the twins. And he just loved to read. Yet he knew that without her, he would starve and be very lonely, so he gave her his full respect. Cambria applied for food stamps, did the grocery shopping, and always made sure there were cooked meals in the household for her siblings. She saw Anisha, the healthy twin off to school and sometimes skipped school to care for Tanisha, the autistic twin. Making visits to the doctor or tending to Tanisha's self-inflicted injuries were the days she dreaded the most.

Momma Keisha was thirty years old. She gave birth to Cambria when she was fifteen, Devontae came when she was seventeen and the twins arrived when she was twenty two. When she found out that one of the twins, Tanisha, had autism, she went into a state of depression. And never quite recovered from the loss of her grandmother. Overcome with grief and feeling as if an evil spirit had cursed death and destruction upon her womb. Youth was no longer a luxury she could afford. She had dropped out of school when she was sixteen and found a job as a cashier. It was close enough to home, so that she could rush over to the house on breaks to check on the kids. Not the best at anything but she had always been a sweet child. Even as an infant, when she realized that her playtime visit to Grandma's house was permanent and her mother never came back to pick her up for school, she was still understanding. 'Momma must have some important business to take care of,' she thought and left it at that. But after the shock of having a special needs child, the abandonment of yet a third baby daddy and the death of her grandmother, she could no longer hide behind the naivety of a child's visor. She was in pain and no one was there to comfort her; not even her children understood. Thus, the addiction began.

Cambria wrapped a large royal blue cloth around her waist and another around her thick, black hair. Making her way to the kitchen, she noticed a fly moving hastily about the room. It frantically tumbled into counters, cabinets and lights and finally plummeting down at her feet. She shook her head and swept him into a glass jar. Then, took the jar outside to let the fly go free. She never liked to see any living thing die for no reason.

Approaching steadily from down the street was a young boy riding his bicycle. It was a tall bike, obviously too big for his small body. Each foot dangled as it waited for the pedal to come back around to the top of its rotation. Then, he pushed it down forcefully and missed the crucial catch of the opposite pedal with his left foot. It caught his ankle and he yelped in agony. She ran to him and brought him to the front steps of her home; held a warm towel to his wound and urged him to be more careful in the future. The screen door opened behind her and a small girl appeared in mismatched shoes; she was smiling but there was a tear drop forming under her right eye, one that refused to fall but looked drastically out of place. The twin was missing her mother; she was smiling because she thought it was her mommy on the front porch and was disappointed when she saw it was only her sister and a strange young boy and so the drop began to form. After applying a bandage, Cambria sent the boy off and entered the house to fix a meal for the girl with the tear drop and her twin, who had wiped the tear away. They ate, quietly. Then, they ran to the ice cream truck that was playing strangely pitched music. The boy joined them and they ate joyously. Cambria retreated to her bedroom and unwrapped her hair. Contemplating washing it, she decided to just sit down and study while the kids were still out playing. Taking off her mommy hat and putting on her student thinking cap. She wondered when their *real* mom would come home and relieve her of this arduous duty.

What did she know of the pleasures of hanging out with those her own age? Exploring the city – within safe boundaries – perhaps a trip to the arcade or a walk to the park? She often wondered how playing an instrument might feel or rollerblading even. Boats seemed like fun too. Surrounded by miles of glistening water with algae that tickled your feet when you jump in for relief from the August heat. Cambria wanted to see and feel the water but settled for an occasional sprinkler run, the grass serving as her algae. And she would imagine her sisters as the exotic fish dressed in bright colors, like those of the Australian coral reef.

But this was no moment for daydreaming; she had a few more daylight hours to be productive. The first math homework question asked, 'If a fisherman has two red fish that sell for $4 each and three blue fish that sell for $10 each. How much money will he make if he sells everything?' And she answered, '2+4+3+10=$19 in total.'

FALLIN

January had come so quickly and most students were itching for Winter Break. One particular Monday, Ms. Ecko's class had an unusual air of excitement. There was an undertone of whispers and short burst of laughter. An onlooker may have heard an occasional 'FOR REAL!' or 'Oh My God' but the actual subject matter was well hidden amidst the chatter. Apparently, Mike, one of the athletic boys, had made it to second base with a girl named Cherie in the other 8th grade homeroom class. It happened after Friday's basketball game, they were kissing behind the gymnasium bleachers and Cherie agreed to give him head but just as she was in the middle of pleasing this highly sought after jock, Mrs. Colts, the principal, walked into the gym and found them. Now, the entire 8th grade class was at risk of being banned from the annual class ski trip in two weeks.

Nawiri was disgusted by the thought of what happened, Sasha was angry about the ski trip and Devontae was amused about the whole situation. He attempted to offer comic relief but Nawiri and Sasha would not laugh. 'I bet she bit down when she heard Mrs. Colts heels storming toward them and that nigga, Mike, was probably screaming like a baby!' They just shook their heads at his foolish speculations. 'Where is the sense? First of all, I never thought Cherie was like that, she seemed like such a sweet girl. Now, she's out here compromising herself for some no good little boy. And what was she thinking anyway that is so nasty,' said Nawiri with a look of disgust.

'I know you not talking about my best friend.' One of the dolls retorted after hearing Nawiri's opinion of the situation. Nawiri paused trying to decide whether or not she wanted to argue with her but she was a few second too slow. Sasha jumped in defensively, 'And so what if she is, what the fuck are you gonna do about it?' The girl was clearly taken aback. 'That's what I thought.' Sasha sat back in her seat.

She was conflicted; she didn't want to tell Nawiri that she wasn't a virgin. That she was molested by her mother's ex-boyfriend and had relations with boys in her neighborhood ever since. More than anyone else, she valued Nawiri's opinion of her, so she pretended that she was also disgusted with Cherie's actions. Cherie's motivations were unknown but Nawiri could only imagine that she probably watched music videos and sex scenes in movies and wanted to please Mike the same way that the girls on television did. But for Sasha, she didn't really have an explanation for her sexual adventures; they seemed to be spontaneous and unemotional. An act that her body was now accustomed to and sometimes yearned for but nothing she could truly explain to anyone else. Even the brush of a hand could arouse her desires and usually she would show up at James' house, down the street from her or Anthony's basement or Brandon's bedroom. Even Devontae sometimes turned her on but she was careful to hide these feelings because she saw the subtle affection that existed between he and Nawiri, even though they had not acknowledged it themselves.

Mrs. Colts gathered the 8th grade class for an emergency assembly during the lunch period. She gave a vague reason why the trip would be tentatively cancelled until further notice. Luckily for the kids, she changed her mind two days later and the trip was back on. Devontae didn't want to show his excitement, especially because his mind was so focused on how he would make the money to pay for the ski rental. He decided to sale a few of his songs to a neighbor for ten dollars each. That would give him enough money for rental and maybe even some hot cocoa for Nawiri, since she always complained of being cold.

The day came and the trio lined up for the bus, ready for an adventure. Carthart jackets. Mittens. Black gloves. Ski masks and skull caps. Water-proof boots. Sweat pants. Snow pants and heating pads. Most kids had found some mixture of the suggested outerwear. Only four students had actually brought snow pants, others came in an assortment of jeans and nylon bottoms. Equipped with skis and poles, the children stumbled out onto the glistening white terrain. The white, wintery hills loomed over them as they looked up, intimidated by the steep slopes and colossal elevation. Nawiri had never seen such a magnificent sight. Devontae and Sasha were more skeptical. Turning from the larger hill, they were relieved when they saw the beginner hill, a smaller white mound of snow that was much less overwhelming. This mound was not as pristine and glistening, it was more of a tannish brown, worn down by the less experienced skiers tracking dirt from the ski lodge. The high traffic had unfortunately melted patches of snow down to the ground. Nevertheless, this was the hill of choice for

99% of the inexperienced skiers, which made up the majority of the skiers on the course. After an hour or so, Nawiri decided that the beginner area was too crowded for her. She snuck away and climbed into a lift that travelled on a moving line above the lodge and past all of the beginner hills, right up to the highest peak. At first, she was filled with excitement. The air was crisp and the challenge was exhilarating, even though she lacked the skills and the necessary preparation. The world looked so beautiful from this vantage point; all of her friends and teachers standing below, became smaller and smaller as she drifted toward the snow-capped peak. She even seemed to forget why she was on the lift, where she came from and how she got there as the anticipation of reaching the top clouded her memory and her perception of reality. But as she neared the pinnacle, anxiety and fear took hold of her nerves. She panicked, looking around for someone to help her get down and back to safe ground. At the peak, someone yelled, telling her to jump off of the lift. Upon impact with the mountain, she found herself already sliding down the mountain before she could even stand up straight. Tears streaming, she held onto a tree for dear life. The few people around her encouraged her to let go and ski down. She cried out in agony, 'I shouldn't be up here, it was a mistake! I can't ski down, I'm too afraid. Please, somebody help me!'

'Sorry darling, we can't help you. We've got to ski down ourselves. All I can tell you is to straighten out your skis, bend your knees and let gravity guide you down. Good luck!' The family skied down and left Nawiri with her deathly fear. She looked around, praying for someone to appear, for some hero to save her. But there was nothing but cold air, gray skies and slippery, melting snow beneath her. Closing her eyes, she let go of the tree and let the white snow slide underneath her skis, when she opened her eyes, the wind was whipping across her face and she was travelling upwards of thirty miles an hour. Once again, panic overtook her and one ski crossed the other bringing her quickly to the ground. She began to tumble rapidly down the hill, trying to shield her face from the sharp tips of the skis. She lost her poles and after what seemed like hours, she landed at the base of the hill. The chaperones and teachers came rushing to her aid. Everyone in the lodge had watched her tumble; pointing and gasping at the terrible and unfortunate fall. They raised her by her armpits only to witness a bloody face, her nose and bottom lip bled while a large bruise formed on her forehead.

Sasha and Devontae were at the top of the beginner hill when they noticed a figure in the distance tumbling down the giant, white mountain. They rushed to the scene with everyone else, squeezing through the colorful medley of jackets and brown faces to find the bloody girl was their beloved companion, Nawiri. They followed the busy crowd into the lodge. Devontae stopped to buy a cup of hot chocolate and motioned for Sasha to continue walking. 'I should have bought this for her earlier, then she wouldn't have been up on that huge hill. What was she thinking?' he thought. When he got to her, she was sitting with one leg propped on a chair, an ice pack was stuck to her head and a napkin covered her nose. Her huge, brown eyes looked up at him as he assessed her condition and he melted with sorrow. His heart was beating heavily as he pulled up a chair to sit down. 'I was looking for you. I bought you some hot chocolate,' he said gently. Her eyes watered, they both knew she couldn't drink the cocoa but she was thankful for the kind gesture regardless. 'I can't believe you went up there, I don't understand you, crazy girl. Scaring us half to death. The average person can only dream of being as daring but please don't ever do that again without at least taking lessons first.'

'Excuse me Devontae, Miss Simmons' ambulance is here. You'll see her at school next week.'

'Ambulance? Is it that serious? I want to go with her!'

'Me too!' Sasha cosigned.

'Sorry kids, that is not allowed.'

Nawiri closed her eyes as they lay her on the stretcher. Devontae thought about how brown and beautiful her eyes had been and how he longed to see them again. He rushed over to the doors, as a last attempt to catch up with her but the paramedics were already loading her onto the ambulance when he got there.

FLASHING LIGHTS

In hindsight, Devontae thought he should have searched for her as soon as he noticed she was missing but he assumed that she had just went into the lodge to use the restroom or to blow her nose, anything but ride the lift up to the highest peak at the resort. Wednesday and Thursday passed and Nawiri didn't show; lunchtime had become awkward. Sasha and Devontae had little to talk about. Sasha was shy and introspective, so he was always forced to initiate the conversation. They sat down at the lunch table and quietly ate, listening to the conversations around them. Sasha's eyes wandered aimlessly about the cafeteria, over crevices and under tables, observing shoes and jewelry, hairdos and mannerisms. Devontae interrupted her silent observations, he wasn't aware of the rapid activity in her brain. She was analyzing and assessing her surroundings, constantly. 'Why are you looking so lost? You got a special boy on your mind?'

'Oh no! I'm sorry, I was just looking around,' she said, embarrassed of how she must have looked in her intense gaze.

'You don't really talk about dudes that much, you got a boyfriend? Why don't you talk to some of the boys around here? They seem smart, not as smart as me! But smart enough and I know you and Nawiri wouldn't have it any other way.'

'I don't know,' she shrugged. 'I went with Johnny for a week in the beginning of the school year but then we broke up because I wasn't really feeling him like that anymore. And then I went with Travis for three weeks in October, which was a long time and I thought it was going good but then I saw him flirting with other girls on the third week, so by that Friday I just couldn't put up with it anymore. That's why I'm trynna stay away from these Century boys now 'cause they are no good, they got too many girls trynna get with them all at the same time. You know what I mean?'

'I guess, but girls aren't all over me like that.'

'That's because you don't pay attention to them but they all talk about how they like you. You're just too wrapped up with Nawiri to notice.'

'Whatchu mean wrapped up? I'm wrapped up in trying to get the most out of this education. Nawiri is cool, I wouldn't say I'm wrapped up, I don't even know what that shit means.'

'Whatever,' Sasha replied, rolling her eyes with a smirk, 'you are so sprung you can't even see it' I think it's cute though. I like that ya'll are taking it slow. I can't do that. I just jump right in and when they piss me off, then I'm on to the next one. That's why I don't even talk about these niggas 'cause I don't even talk to them long enough to really tell anybody except Nawiri. I tried talking to one boy at a time, now I'm just like whatever. I can play the game better than they can.'

'Humph, you females are so complicated. I like to keep things nice and simple.'

'You like to keep things nice and Nawiri!'

'Where are you gettin' this from?' he replied, irritated. Sasha was amused, only time would tell if her speculations were right.

Friday came and Devontae decided that since Nawiri had been so good to him when he was missing school and not performing well that he would take the pre-algebra and natural science homework to her house. Sasha gave him directions and he hopped on the bus after school. It was a beautiful, sunny day, the bitter cold made the sun hard to appreciate but he did anyway. As he looked out of the window, he saw gas stations, beauty supply stores, liquor stores, barber shops, daycare centers, storefront churches, and of course two McDonald's, a Kentucky Fried Chicken, Wendy's, Pizza Hut, Little Caesars, Chuck's Soul Food and Avalon Bakery. He got off of the bus at Seven Mile and Livernois Ave. Walking down Seven Mile, he came to her street sign, Gloucester Drive, turned left and stopped dead in his tracks.

At this moment in time, his world began to spin out of control. He couldn't decide if he had stepped into a matrix-like dream world or if this was in fact reality that was captivating all of his senses. Never in his life had he seen such beautiful homes, heard about them yes, but seeing them with his own eyes was a mystical experience. Unconsciously, Devontae's feet began to move, one in front of the other, his eyes glued to the majestic wonderland of colonial style columns and brick tutor mansions that enclosed him.

‘This is ridiculous! What do people do with all of this space? How did they even get enough money to pay for this shit? I bet they all dope dealers, athletes and rappers like my man Jay-Z. Dang, that one look like a medieval castle from the 1600s. Cape Coast style. I wonder if they Black. Gotta be, it’s Detroit. Maybe not though, rich niggas would put metal bars in front of these carved oak doors with dead bolts for extra security.’ Devontae mumbled to himself. He wanted so badly to know what it was like to live in a home like these. To shower in the marble floor bathrooms and sit by the large fireplaces in the winter while sipping hot cocoa, to play on the outdoor playscapes in the backyards and swim in the aqua blue pools in the summer. He thought of how he could have friends come over and not be ashamed of the meagerness, the simplicity. His emotions quickly shifted from awe to anger.

After what seemed like hours of slowly walking through a confusing maze of winding streets, giant pine trees and many styles of fences, he came to 514 Gloucester Drive. He was hoping that Nawiri’s house would be less grandiose than the others, just a little closer to his own reality, so that he would not feel intimidated or jealous but to his dismay it was just as beautiful and amazing as the others and equally as infuriating. Standing awkwardly at the intersection of the sidewalk and the walkway leading to their door, he forgot why he was there and turned to leave. Suddenly, a voice called out to him, startled, he turned back around looking for a face he recognized.

‘Hey there, I saw you looking at the house, can I help you with something young man?’ Ms. Heath projected from behind the screen door.

‘Oh, I was, uh, well, I came, so that, um…’ Devontae was hopelessly tongue-tied.

‘Are you here to see Nawiri, son?’

Devontae’s eyes were wide with fear, he no longer wanted to be there and wished he had never come. He wanted more than anything to run in the opposite direction and never set foot again on the streets with houses that laughed at him and mocked his poverty.

‘No, I was just going. I just stopped in front to admire your beautiful home.’

But before he could make a run for it, he heard Nawiri calling his name. ‘Devontae? Devontae! Is that you? You came all the way here to see me and won’t come in? G’Ma!! Tell him to come back!’

Devontae was confused. ‘How did she even see me?’ he thought.

‘Come back, young man.’ Ms. Heath ordered. ‘You can eat dinner with us, there’s enough food for everyone!’

Devontae walked toward the house drudgingly, the voices in his head telling him to run, while his body disobeyed.

Inside the foyer, warmth, luscious smells, and bright, yellow lights flooded his senses. The stimuli was intense, just shy of overwhelming but the allure was so inviting that he wished he could stay forever.

The floors in the entrance hallway, den and dining room were solid red oak. The living room had a plush, tan carpet and from what he could see, the kitchen had a tan tile floor with granite countertops and steel appliances that had all retained their shining store display quality, just like those he had seen in the Home Depot. Each room was painted a different color; it was a peculiar feature that he had never seen. The living room was a brownish orange, the den had light brown walls and the dining room was a pastel yellow. As they toured each room, he felt his mood changed with the colors. Some rooms were bright, others had dim lighting that made him feel sleepy. The most extraordinary part of his journey throughout the house were the decorations, exotic ornaments, pictures of flowers and wild animals, beautiful Black Princesses and slaves, strange symbols for which he did not know the meaning, candles and brilliant baskets, clay pots and potpourri, ivory stone statues, blown glass vases and modern furniture with unique shapes and defined lines. When he looked up, the ceilings told their own story; he could make out abstract figures on the textured surfaces and miniature gargoyles stared back at him from the corners of the wall. The chandelier in the dining room hung low, light reflecting off of each crystal and refracting back into his dazed eyes.

'Have a seat at the table, Devontae, is it?' Ms. Heath asked politely.

'Yes, thank you Ma'am.'

‘I’ll go grab Nawiri, she still isn’t strong enough to walk.’

Ms. Heath entered the room with her granddaughter’s small frame folded neatly in her arms and her head propped up with a wide smile. Nawiri looked like a princess, as she observed her visitor with great affection in her eyes.

‘I can’t believe you walked all the way here to see me,’ she exclaimed cheerfully.

‘I didn’t walk, I took the bus,’ Devontae replied.

‘Well you had to walk when you got off the bus, didn’t you?’

‘Yeah, I guess.’

‘Right, see you always got something smart to say.’

‘No, that’s you.’

Ms. Heath stood listening to the light bickering between the two, laughed, then disappeared into the kitchen.

‘You, uh, um, you…’

‘What?! You what?!’ Nawiri replied playfully.

‘You look better than I expected. It looks like your wounds are healing fast. That’s good,’ said Devontae, trying not to sound too impressed by her healthy glow.

‘Thank you, I think my positive attitude is speeding up my recovery,’ Nawiri raised her eyebrows, amused with her own sophisticated intuition about healing. Devontae's wounds had also been healing, for months his routine of alcohol swabs, shea butter and cocoa butter seemed to be paying off. Even his posture was almost back to normal.

They laughed lightly, like strangers. Nawiri had never imagined what it would be like to see Devontae outside of school, especially not in her own house. So, she wasn't quite sure how to respond to his presence here, in her dining room.

'You have a beautiful home, I can only imagine how it must feel to live in a big ass crib like this!' Devontae exclaimed, surprised at his own honesty.

'It's just a house, protects us from the rain. I think most houses serve the same purpose. Ours just has a few extra rooms and interior decorations for aesthetic purposes.'

'Interior decorations for aesthetic purposes,' Devontae mocked Nawiri, wobbling his head and piercing his lips in imitation of her prim and proper disposition.

Ms. Heath walked into the room, interrupting Nawiri's retaliation to his mockery. She held a large platter of baked chicken seasoned with thyme and rosemary. The legs, breasts, wings and thighs looked tender and juicy. The aroma drifted up through their nostrils and the honey glaze making their mouth's water. Next were the vegetable bowls - tossed spinach salad, steamed broccoli and baked sweet potatoes. The food was just as luxurious as the house. Devontae couldn't remember the last time he had eaten a full meal with every food group, such as the one sitting before him. Reluctant to touch the food, not wanting to destroy the lovely display, Devontae waited for a signal. Ms. Heath pleaded for him to dig in and he submitted without hesitation. G'Ma and Nawiri followed his lead. Ms. Robyn was working late, as usual.

It is a wonder the thoughts that are constructed by young minds and the feelings that well up in innocent hearts. Devontae walked home in an unsettled cloud of emotion. The warmth from the flavorful meal settled in his stomach and the sweet voices resonated in his ears. Nawiri's glow, despite her weakened body, was more astounding than ever and the ambiance of the home sealed the experience.

But fury was rattling his bones and growing swiftly from his root chakra[2]. Wispy thoughts of adoration were gradually replaced with devious plots of advancement. Devontae fixed his mind around the thought of selling Marijuana. He thought, 'If I sell ten dime bags a day, pay my distributor one-third, spend a third on nice things, like what Nawiri and her Moms got, and save the last third, I'll be on their level by the time I'm fifty. But I'll have had so many bills by the time I'm fifty that all the money I save will be gone. Dang, I need to sale Crack and Heroin and maybe even them pills the white kids be poppin', then I'll be on that level next week! Rollin' in dough, call me Pillsbury dope boy.'

---

[2] The root chakra is located at the base of the spine at the tailbone in back, and the pubic bone in front. This center holds the basic needs for survival, security and safety.

Devontae tossed around ideas, thought of the people he needed to speak with for more information about the drug game and calculated how much time it would take him to accumulate the amount of wealth necessary for him to live in Nawiri's neighborhood, purchase artwork like theirs, eat delicious food and enjoy life accordingly. Just picturing the amount of money he could make a day, selling drugs, made his heart beat faster with excitement and pleasure. And then he stopped dead in his tracks, remembering.

He could see his mother, begging for a hit, offering her body to different men, selling her soul for a quick high. He could see other moms doing the same, fathers, brothers, sisters destroying themselves and their families. He could see his younger sisters crying after five days without their mother home, wondering if she is dead or alive. Right then, he decided that he could not be the one responsible for that type of pain. He would rather die, starving in an ally, than to destroy his own family and others like theirs.

Once again, he was back to the drawing board.

RUNAWAY

The trees began to whisper night time secrets as the sun set on the horizon. The Northeast wind kicked up tiny rocks and sand from the baseball diamond. Swings rattled in their emptiness as the wind set them in motion and the monkey bars turned frigid. Spring was approaching but snow-filled February nights were still unfriendly to the average school child, who was raging with energy and yearning to be on the playground with friends. The previous night, Trey Donovan's tongue was stuck to the frosted railroad tracks. This was no weather for child's play. He had been trying to impress none other than Sasha Gordon with his mischievous courage but Sasha's mind was elsewhere.

Every house was lit with bright, soft white lights. Fireplaces were left untouched; electric heaters and furnaces had made the people lazy. They sat in their family rooms watching Martin and Fresh Prince of Belaire, The Cosby's, E.R., and B.E.T. After dinner, the lights went out, the televisions were switched off and the children were put to bed.

She slid out of the frozen window with ease. It wasn't the first time and it wouldn't be the last. The wind whipped her face relentlessly and her hot sauce stained fingers stung from the cold, so she clenched her fists. The snow lifted and swirled in circles making miniature typhoons, the metal fences swayed and shutters flapped open and closed. Even the moon seemed to be blinking its eyes, playing peek-a-boo with the world behind thick, gray clouds. It cast a glow on the dark corridors and alleyways of the Conner Creek district, providing light for nighttime pedestrians. She slipped into an old 1976 Ford Mustang. The rusty parts were no longer fit for travel. The car had been out of commission since 1992, sitting on bricks. The green paint was peeling excessively; some would even argue that the car was actually blue yet the sun had blazed a way for a new existence. She opened her legs wide. Nothing about the car seemed to merit such a long stay, taking up valuable and useable space in a crowded back yard with lawn mowers, abandoned toys, cigarette butts, machine shop tools and clothes that never made their way to the Salvation Army. She bit down on her lower lip and endured the first jolt of pain. The park stood silently across the street, everything was still with the exception of the whispering trees. The second jolt was less bearable and the third was even worse. A tear dropped onto the leather seat. Those leather seats had lasted despite the shanty exterior, the seats were still soft and they even retained some of their original polished quality. A few cracks here and there but otherwise, they were as good as new. Finally, the shadow above her had reached his climax and was done with her body. She opened the door, to weather the storm once more, making her way home silently, trying to avoid the moon and the whispering trees. She bent her knees to relinquish the pain but her emotional turmoil remained heavy and unsettled.

Sasha was sitting in the living room window, missing Nawiri and watching cars pass by. Thought about going to visit her best friend but reclined after a lazy attempt to stand. She held a pen and a blank sheet of paper, searching for poetic inspiration.

Life is a mystery to me

Looking for love in the emptiest sea

*Niggas ain't s*** and my Momma is a b*****

Why can't I find anyone to love me?

They all want to know how I can be of use

The only person who cares is my best friend from school

What is the point, I'm living for nothing

Pretty feet walking in uncomfortable shoes

I'm a mess,

So if this is a test

God, please tell me how to pass

Sasha searched for love in the streets to make up for the lack of love she received in the household. Her mind was full of math, science, English and Social Studies lessons but no amount of education or late night escapades with older boys could make up for the emptiness in her heart. It was a start – the poetry – self-healing in a world where children's problems were often overlooked and ignored. But was it enough?

'Nawiri's life is perfect,' she thought. 'No drama, No niggas, No crazy Momma, No shared room or threatening objects being thrown at her.

She is so lucky. Why me? I must have done something wrong. But what was it? Maybe I shouldn't have peed on myself that one time in Kindergarten. Momma was real mad about that. I got that light skin too, maybe I'm payin' for that. Oh my God, I did drop Niamako on the head that one time when she was a baby. But I swear, I didn't think anybody saw that. Damn, maybe I do deserve this misery.'

Outside, the trees reminded her of the previous night. They never missed an opportunity to remind her. The only living things awake at all times of the day and night, watching over the curious two-legged and four-legged creatures around them.

She drifted into a light sleep for a moment and then awoke to the sound of heavy shoes, clanging keys, bags hitting the walls and her mother's thunderous roar as she rampaged down the stairs, ready for battle.

EMPIRE STATE OF MIND

'Ooooo, weee!! It smells so good in here!!' Cambria exclaimed. 'Whatchu cookin' up in here? I want some, whatever it is.'

She walked into the kitchen searching for the source of the luscious aroma. When she sighted his plate, she gasped, 'Ugh! What the hell is that? You in here eatin' grass? And what is that mushy stuff, it looks spoiled. Where you get this from? I know you ain't cook this.'

'It's leftovers from a friend's house damn, why you gotta come breathin' all over my food with yo' dragon breath.'

'Whatever, my breath is probably gonna make that monkey food taste good. I'm 'bout to make some noodles.'

'Haha, you mean you 'bout to put some water in that cup of salty ass noodles and stir for approximately sixty seconds, then eat it in approximately fifteen seconds.'

'You a salty ass noodle. When you get too good for Raman? Boy please, you'll be eating this tomorrow for dinner.'

Cambria continued to talk about Devontae's uncharacteristically healthy meal but he tuned out her voice. He was still in deep thought about how he could make enough money to afford a life of luxury like Nawiri's. It didn't occur to him that Ms. Robyn had worked many years to accumulate enough money for her house and that her ex-husband had also contributed to purchasing the home. Devontae figured if he could just hustle smart that he would have enough money for at least a down payment in three years.

All the boys on the block had been shooting dice since they were seven and eight years old. Devontae knew how to play but had never been any good at it. His heart lie in books but for this new money-making mission, he decided he would try his hand at it again.

Cambria fidgeted around the kitchen, looking for a clean fork. Then decided to wash dishes because it was taking too long to find a clean utensil. She gathered all of the plates, pots, utensils, and empty cups and threw them in the sink, filled it with soapy water, all the while mumbling about the lack of help she received around the house from lazy siblings. Devontae finished his plate, placed it in the sink and headed out into the windy street. Cambria smacked her lips, thinking a chore sheet was long overdue.

The beginning of March brought some relief from the snow but little respite from the cold. On days like this, one could usually find all of the young boys inside of Thomas Shepard's house. They would make a large circle in the basement and play late into the night. He knocked on the door apprehensively but there was no reply. Rocking from heel to toe, he waited impatiently. Then, he rang the doorbell. A woman's voice yelled from inside, 'Who is it?!'

'Devontae, from down the street!' He yelled back, through the closed door.

The door opened and a robust woman answered, filling the doorway. She had smooth, oily skin that glowed from sweat that had formed a thin layer over her face. Her stomach protruded so far that he thought she might be pregnant. Her weave looked like a wild bush and her hands were covered in grease. From the smell, he assumed that she had been frying chicken or catfish. Either way, her large frame and unwelcoming stare intimidated him, so he entered the house and walked toward a door that looked like it would lead him to the basement.

'Where the heck you goin'? That's a closet boy. Damn kids just walk up in the house like they know where they goin'.'

'Sorry ma'am, which door is it?' he asked politely.

'The one on the left, it's not that many doors in here. Process of the elimination! And don't trip now, there's a stair missing.'

'This was a good day for you to come,' she continued, 'they bettin' big money down there, I hope you ready!'

Devontae made his way cautiously down the stairs. He could hear the animated shouts from boys his age and some old heads. They looked up with confused and contorted faces; he could tell they were surprised to see him.

'What?!?! Nigga, how you feelin'? I meant to come by the house when you got shot but you know a Nigga stay busy!'

Before he could respond, everyone was saying 'What's up!' and offering their condolences for his injuries. Dap was exchanged in every direction. He hated this part of greetings, touching hands that most likely had not been washed within the past two hours. Big hands, small hands, soft hands, hard hands, and gritty hands. He wiped his palm on his pants leg and moved further into the light. There was a pile of money on a dusty pool table and a worn pair of dice.

'You remember how to play dog? I know it's been a minute. Watch how a pro shoots his dice,' boasted Keith, who was known for being a ladies man and not the best at craps.

There were only four players, the rest stood around shouting support, making side bets and passing Henessy. A couple of them had retreated to a corner to roll a joint but the place was damp, so they were having a hard time lighting it.

Keith rolled snake eyes and lost, then he mumbled something under his breath as he passed the dice along to Junior.

Junior blew on the dice and whispered, 'Come on seven. Come on eleven. Come on seven. Come on eleven.' But he rolled a three instead and crapped out.

Next, Ike threw the dice and rolled an eight. Then, he rolled a seven, which also put him out of the game. He shouted curses and complained about the dice being weighted. Most of the younger boys had their money on Young John and the older boys were betting against him. There was much money at stake, so the room went silent with anticipation.

Young John held the dice, whispering small prayers and proverbs, as he shook them for good luck!! As he threw the dice, everyone instinctively leaned forward and confirmed that a ten had been rolled. The younger boys became nervous because they doubted that Young John would hit his point. And the older ones just chuckled knowing that they were about to win big but Young John was whispering his magical prayer again and threw the dice with surprising confidence. When he rolled another ten, everyone was in disbelief, the ones who had bet on him quickly collected money from their opponents.

The commotion didn't last for long. Mike suggested that Devontae be put in the game next.

'How you gon' tell us who to put in? You see I was up next!' yelled Keith, who was desperate to play again to win some of his money back.

'Man, just relax, let the boy get in the game, he just got out the hospital. The man just got off crutches! Been spending all his money on medical bills and shit, come on!' responded Mike, who had been like an older brother to Devontae when he was younger.

'Aight, fine! But ain't nobody else jumping in front of me!' His face enlivened with anger.

'Ok man, chill,' Mike turned to Devontae, 'show us what you got!'

No one really wanted to bet on Devontae since he was so rusty with the game. Everyone knew that shooting dice was about luck, and this little crippled kid didn't look like he had much luck on side.

So, he stepped into the circle, feeling the intensity around him. Heavy breathing, heavy drinking and heavy smoking occluded his senses. When he picked up the dice, the room began spinning as if it was he himself who was being tossed onto the pool table. Even intense competition in school had never been as thrilling as this. Money made the game feel like life and death were on the table. He decided to risk it all, a stupid yet bold move, he placed one hundred down to bet and another hundred down for a side bet. If he won, he chose life and if he lost, he chose death by his sister's hands. He closed his eyes and the game began. Visions of leprechauns and pots of gold, pirates and hidden treasures, CEOs and Multi-National Corporations came to mind as he focused on rolling winning numbers. With an insatiable thirst for that paper, that bread, them Dead Presidents, he willed all of his energy toward the release, the flight and the landing of the dice. It was a pivotal moment in time, where his thirst for knowledge was overtaken by a fierce competitiveness – for that green paper.

To his surprise and to everyone else's, he actually rolled a seven and won. That night, he came out with one thousand dollars. It was the happiest day of his life. He hobbled home, tears of joy running down his face, thinking about his savings plan.

He wondered if he could manage both - the pursuit of knowledge and of money. He was afraid to sacrifice his soul and conscience for something material and knew that selling drugs would only turn his heart into a cold place, leaving no room for love. And the brain, one dimensional, no room for logic. He figured shooting dice was a safer route to travel.

Half way down the street someone yelled out to him, 'Hey man, are you working hard or hardly working?!' He responded with a winded smile, 'Nigga, I'm hardly working!' Easy money was treating him well – for now.

Still on Cloud Nine, he froze in his living room, surprised to see his mother sprawled out on the couch. Contemplating whether or not to put a blanket over her, he decided not to. It was five a.m. and he knew she would explode, if she knew how late he had stayed out. He also didn't want her to know how much money he had won. Shutting the door softly, he made his way up the stairs and entered his room. Cambria came in quietly behind him.

'Where the hell have you been? You got me up worried sick and I need to be at school in two hours. Where is the money I loaned you?' she snapped at him in a motherly tone.

'I got you plus interest. Three hundred dollars. Go buy yourself something nice.' Devontae whispered, smartly. He handed her the money, grinning with pride at his accomplishment.

'Are you kidding? Have you seen the twins' clothing. They are too small; they have holes. If anything, I'll buy something for them first. Anyway, don't even come home next time you decide to stay out until five, punk!' Cambria walked back to her bedroom with her hand on her hip as if she was feeling aches and pains. Her responsibilities seemed to be aging her far beyond her years. She curled into a fetal position, trying to put herself back to sleep as her brother shuffled through his closet in the next room for the perfect shoe box to hide his money.

The next day, Devontae was too tired to go to school. He woke up around noon and went downstairs to the kitchen to fix a bowl of cereal. Momma Kiesha, Cambria and the twins had all gone out. He thought about going to the library to read up on gambling but hadn't made up his mind before he heard a knock at the door.

He opened the front door slowly, only to find Junior dressed and ready to explore the world. 'Damn dog, how you get up so early? I'm still tired from last night,' said Devontae.

'Nigga, it's a new day, gotta get paid. You lookin' like you got hit by a train. What you doin' today?'

'I don't know yet.' Devontae said sleepily, wiping crust out of his eye and taking another spoonful of Cocoa Puffs.

'Well, you should come hang with us. You be actin' too good to role wit' a nigga.'

'Man, I got school' Devontae said defensively.

'I got school too.'

‘But you don’t do shit. What’s the point of being in school if you never go and when you do go, you clown?’

‘I don’t know, the females, I guess. I mean the shit is easy, if I wanted to do good then I could, I just don’t try,’ Junior shrugged. Devontae could not even count the number of times he had heard the same statement come out of so many of his friend’s mouths. It was like they had gathered in a meeting of thousands and rehearsed it perfectly, so that none of them could ever forget the reason why they didn’t do well in school.

‘But anyway,’ Junior continued, ‘you should come freestyle with us. We all do better when you there cause you raise the bar.’

‘I don’t know, I might. Where ya’ll meeting at?’

‘At John’s crib.’

‘Alright, I’ll probably be over there in a few hours.’

‘Ok, cool.’ Junior walked away, flipping a swisher between his fingers, bouncing a basketball in the other hand. He hummed the chorus from Biggie’s ‘Mo’ Money Mo’ Problems.’ Then turned back and yelled, ‘Man, you better come dog!’ Then, headed to the corner store with his taste buds set on some Better Made Barbeque chips.

Devontae shut the door and took a spoon full of cereal. The living room was a mess, it looked as if someone had turned it upside down and emptied out all of the hidden contents. The cushions and pillows from the worn couch were on the floor. The china cabinet drawers were open and a few of the dusty glasses were shattered on the floor. Some of the pictures on the walls were tilted sideways. 'Was there an earthquake last night, damn?' Devontae thought.

Suddenly, he dropped his bowl and jolted up the stairs skipping one or two steps at a time. Milk from the bowl flew up in the air, defying gravity and splattering his legs and feet but he didn't care. He went straight to the spot where last night's profit was hidden. Heart palpitating thunderously in his chest, he opened the shoe box slowly. When he opened his eyes, the empty box was only visible for a few seconds before he smashed the box against the wall. Momma Kiesha had stolen his money. 'WHAT THE FUCK?!! God Damn it!! That Bitch!! I can't believe this shit!' he yelled in agony. 'Why me God? Why? What the hell did I do to deserve this?' His small frame sunk to the floor as he felt a piercing bolt of hatred shoot through his heart. Hate for the world, hate for disparity, hate for suffering, hate for poverty, hate for addiction. Yet, he resisted feeling hate toward his mother; thinking of her more as a victim of her own circumstance. 'She is so weak,' he thought. 'How can you steal from your own kids?' He sat for a long time, shaking with anger, wondering if his life would always be this challenging; if he would go to college; how he would pay for it; if he could ever work his way out of poverty; if he would be forced to do it illegally; what the consequences might be; where his father was; if he had other siblings; if his father loved those kids more than him; if his Grandmother was still alive and where she could possibly be; where his mother was and what was she doing; how his money was being spent; if he would ever have enough to buy a house big enough to impress a girl like Nawiri.

At 3:30pm, Cambria walked into his room after school, surprised to see her little brother with his head between his knees. 'What are you doing in here on the floor? Lookin' pitiful as hell, like a sad little puppy dog.' Cambria teased.

'Momma stole my money!' he exclaimed.

'Oh, right. No, Momma almost stole your money. I saw her tearin' up the living room this morning, so I ran up here and grabbed your money before I went to school. I just got back from the bank; I opened an account for you. You not gonna be able to take the money out until you're eighteen but for now, you can put in as much as you want. So, next time you make some money, don't bring it home, just take it straight to the bank. See Lil'man, I got your back. You think just cause I don't spend all day reading like you that I don't have no sense. Well, ya' thought wrong. Here is all the information about the account. Keep it somewhere safe.' Cambria turned to leave.

'Cambria wait.'

She turned around, 'What?'

Devontae stood up and gave his sister a long, powerful hug. It was so real and so sincere that it brought tears to her eyes. She had to push him away. Wiping her face, she said, 'I know we didn't ask for this life but we have to stay strong, there's no other choice.' It was moments like these that kept them dedicated to one another and to keeping the family together. She turned abruptly and walked back down the stairs to prepare dinner, there was no time to be emotional.

Devontae took a few deep breaths, jumped in the shower and headed out the door to John's house to join the freestyle session.

When he arrived, they had already been at it for an hour. Junior was battling Ike:

I don't carry glocks but you'll catch me doing dishes

Think it's funny homie, next you'll catch me witcha Misses

Not sayin' I'm a beast but just know that I'll eat ya

Cook ya up fa dinner but you smelling like my feces

Feed you to the dogs, now I'm on to the next one

Nigga wanna step up, betta know you gonna catch one

'Devontae, you gotta get in on this one. Junior is getting good, he can give you a run for your money,' exclaimed Young John. The beat boxing started and Devontae tuned in intently.

Niggas shot me in the chest, niggas shot me in the leg

Shoulda shot me in the head, if they wanted me dead

I'm a master of deception, a man with three eyes

And my sixth sense is tellin' me that ya flow is bout to die

When you spit your verse, it's like suffocation

Breathing in burnt garbage from incineration

I'm a loyal man, always true to my word

So, when I say you wack, it's the truth, you heard?

‘Dammnnnnn! You gon’ take that Junior?!?!’ said John trying to add fuel to the battle. Junior focused in, feeling the beat, tapping his foot on the ground.

My nigga think he hard cause he got shot by accident

Nobody want you dead but yo’ flow just asked for it

When I get done, you gon’ need some aspirin

I’m bout spit some ill, straight up nasty shit

You think you young Tupac? Well, I’m Biggie reincarnated

Let me introduce you to my world, Nigga, I – made it

Get up in ya’ head nigga, got you feelin’ violated

Knock you out the game, giving you choices and shit

Do you wanna take a beating now or a later lil’ bitch?

‘Awwww, that was sick!!! You got a comeback Devontae??? Man, you gon’ let him punk you like that?’ asked Young John.

This nigga steady recycling the twenty words he knows

Ain’t read a book since preschool, got the choppiest flow

I’m like a tornado in the winter, a lyrical disaster

Only fourteen but I’m feeling like a Kung Fu master

It seems to me that I’m indefinitely underestimated by my enemies

I seek the probability of the possibility of you following me

It is evident that I’m sicker than you, so you need to admit the truth

And actually Tupac was learning from me, I was even a beast in the womb

'Damn man,' said Junior, 'I'm not even gonna hate, that was sweet. You ain't have to come at my reading level though,' he said frowning.

'You know it's all love fam, no disrespect,' responded Devontae. 'Ya'll niggas ain't talkin' bout smoking though.'

'Man, I been rollin' this joint through yo' whole last verse, come on,' said Young John. They stepped outside onto the front porch, the cold air was deceiving as the setting sun had cast a red glow onto the street and into the living room windows, making them forget about the brisk climate. Young John passed to Devontae and he drew hard, sucking green goodness, herbal bliss, and euphoria in and breathing earth-bound problems, worries and concerns out. They sat quietly and reflectively, rigid with occasional shivers. Red eye veins becoming increasingly visible. Minds travelling to further, unknown and mystical places. The universe was open for exploration.

'Man, you ever think about the point of it all?' asked Junior.

'Yeah, nigga,' Devontae laughed, 'all the time.'

'What you mean, Junior?' asked John, frankly.

'I mean how life is so stupid. What the fuck does any of this shit mean? It's all pointless – society, all these systems and industries. All niggas really need is food, water and shelter at the end of the day and I guess clothes too. But all this extra shit, I'm not convinced, man.'

'I feel you dawg but check it - u ain't gon' eat if you don't participate in the system. You feel me?' retorted John.

'Unless, I create my own system.'

'But what makes your system any better than the one that already exists besides the fact that you control it?' asked Devontae.

'Cause nigga, I don't want to be controlled, so my shit not gon' be controlling. Just some straight chill, growing vegetables and herbs for the fam, community schools with small classes and teachers who live in the community. Teaching black history back to 100,000 years ago and shit. Trade schools and universities on every corner of Detroit. We gon' evict every store front church and put in a job corps or a lounge where niggas can go chill and feel free to build. Basically, in my society, muthafuckers will be so empowered they won't need to be controlled. I feel like it ain't really living if somebody else is always controlling what I do.'

'Ok man that all sounds good but you talkin' about education this, education that and yo' ass don't even go to school,' Devontae laughed at his friend.

'Nigga, I don't go because they not teaching about things that are relevant to my life right now. They got us memorizing shit with no application. It's a dead end road to me. I'd rather self-educate than sit around like a zombie listening to them talk nonsense.'

'Dawg, you not reading, you not writing, you not out here shadowing no plumbers, electricians, or barbers, you literally sit in your grandma living room watching television. Which is they most effective way of controlling people, so what the fuck are you talking about? You talking but you not doing shit.' John was getting annoyed with Junior's rhetoric.

'Can a nigga dream, damn? I know man, I'm about to get it together though. But not on no school shit.'

'I feel you man, do what you do. But don't be a hypocrite like the rest of these jokers. I like you're ideas though, there's just no easy solutions,' Devontae lamented, starting to daydream about his future house.

'Solution to what though? Why does everything need to be solved? Maybe some shit we just don't need to understand.'

'But the more you understand, the more life will make sense to you. That's why I'm always reading cause the more I know, the more I realize how much I don't know. And it drives me to keep learning. But if I don't know shit, then I'm gonna believe that I know everything and it'll all be confusing. It's a paradoxical mystery.'

'Ok, D, you just took it too far. All I'm saying is you can know a lot of shit and still be a slave. And I don't wanna be a slave to the system. Let's go back inside, I'm cold as hell. Fingers feelin' like popsicles n' shit.'

'Yeah, well maybe knowledge will inspire the revolution.'

'Yeah, maybe dawg, maybe.'

Debt before jobs, just by the nature of the system. They could feel the pressure – like that of chains – closing in on their freedom. Perhaps it was the high walls around the complex, the metal bars enclosing the windows, the shot gun sitting patiently behind the kitchen door, or the cashier jobs that awaited them. The ones that would pay the rent, maybe the bills but were hardly enough for the food. Money signifying debt just by accumulation. Cheap labor designed by twenty men bent on world domination. Mental, social and economic freedom was not in these young black boys' favor.

They went on freestyling for an hour or so until Devontae became desperately hungry. He left, reluctantly, to go home and see what Cambria had cooked for dinner.

THUGZ MANSION

The days were getting longer; Spring was a time of growth and transformation. The green tips of early tulips were peaking up above the school grounds. Teachers were glad to let the children outside for lunch periods although they hated to deal with the resulting wood chip splinters and concrete injuries. Mrs. Thorp's seventh grade science class began to till their outdoor garden. They were excited to harvest the vegetables for the big soup festival at the end of the school year. Spirits were high. Even the teachers seemed to be in better moods, conversing in louder voices and letting the kids get away with more mischief. Spring had an essence of forgetfulness – teachers would forget that they were angry, forget why they had been irritated, forget about intended suspensions and detentions, parents would forget to pack lunches, forget to check homework, forget about piano practice, kids were forgetting their pencils, forgetting their coats, and forgetting how to act. Everyone's mind was distracted by the changes outdoors.

Nawiri was the only one still one hundred percent present. She felt she needed to make up for the two months of school that she had missed even though she did all of her assignments from home. She had already been back for three weeks but still was not satisfied with the amount of progress she was making. Her class ranking had dropped from number one to number three.

At lunch, Nawiri and Sasha were discussing the upcoming skating party when Devontae sat down with his tray.

'Hey, what's up?' Devontae asked.

'Nothing much, we were just talking about the skating party. I am so excited, I love to skate!' exclaimed Nawiri.

'Yeah, me too but I don't have enough money this time. They are killing me with all of these expensive ass field trips,' expressed Sasha.

'Don't worry girl, I got you,' assured Nawiri.

'Oh, you got her, huh?' asked Devontae, with a smirk on his face.

'Yeah, you got a problem with it? I can pay for you too, if you want.'

'What makes you think that I can't afford it? You don't know nothin' about me.'

'Well, I do know some things, maybe not everything, geesh. But it's not my fault that you're so secretive,' said Nawiri defensively.

'Rich kids just running around throwin' money in the air like it grows on trees.'

'Why do you always have to bring up how much money I have? I actually don't have anything. I live off of my mom's money. She pays the bills, not me. So, maybe your beef is with her, not me.'

'Maybe it's not your money but you are still spoiled as hell.'

'You know what, I'm sick of your shit! Money does not define me! It really hurts my feelings that you think that I'm some kind of spoiled rich kid, who doesn't appreciate anything! I swear I'm not like that but you keep trying to make me into that kind of person and I don't understand why!' This was the second time that Nawiri had gone off on Devontae, the first being in detention. She always felt relieved for sticking it to him but also guilty because despite her confusion, she had a feeling that his attitude toward her had something to do with his own insecurities. She just didn't have the evidence to back up her suspicions.

'Whatever,' Devontae stood up from the table without having touched his food, 'I'm 'bout to go play football. Peace.'

'Fine! Go play your ol' stanky football, we don't need you over here!' Nawiri yelled. She would have been flush red, if her skin was lighter, instead her ebony complexion hid her frustration. Hands shaking, Nawiri tried to finish her lunch but it was useless.

On her way to the car after school, Nawiri crossed paths with Devontae, who was walking home. He looked at her and ignored her waving hand, then fixed his eyes on a pole in the distance and continued walking straight ahead. Nawiri was usually patient with Devontae's mood swings but this time she refused to cater to him. 'He is acting like such a baby,' she thought as she slid into her mother's Mercedes and drove past him. Splashing water on his uniform shoes.

When Devontae got home, Cambria came out of the kitchen and met him in the living room.

'Hey! How was your day?' she asked politely, as she wiped her hands on a kitchen towel, with blue checkers.

'It was straight. How was yours?' asked Devontae, placing his backpack on the floor.

'Straight too,' Cambria responded, smiling. He didn't like the look of her smile; it was so forced that it seemed more like a grimace. He hated when she tried to play Mommy, greeting him at the door with her oven mittens and apron on, like Betty Crocker. There was no better reminder of their situation than her kitchen wear but he didn't want to seem unappreciative, so he just played along as best he could.

'Aye, I forgot to tell you this morning; I made five hundred dollars last night at Young John's house!' exclaimed Devontae.

Momma Kiesha came running out of the kitchen, he hadn't realized she was home and was shocked to see her in the day time. It had been so long since he had seen her during the day.

'What did you just say boy?' asked his mother in an animated tone, eyes wide with excitement.

'Nothin', I just said I ate five hundred calories last night at Young John's house. I'm trying to gain weight to try out for the Police Athletic League football team next year. You would know that if you were here more often,' he said with a frown.

‘I knew that, don’t disrespect me! I’m still yo’ mama.’ She walked back to the kitchen, embarrassed for her intrusion and for her lack of knowledge about what was going on in her own household. They could hear her in the kitchen rambling on, ‘I’m still your mother. This is still my house.’

The twins were sitting on the couch watching cartoons, as usual. Cambria had given them fruit roll-ups, so they were consumed with licking their sticky fingers and squirming around on the couch, repositioning themselves to see the television around Devontae and Cambria, who were blocking their view.

‘Why don’t ya’ll go outside and play?’ he asked Anisha.

‘Cause this is my favorite show!’ replied Anisha, frowning as she tore off a piece of her fruit roll-up.

Becoming increasingly annoyed by the presence of everyone around him, he walked back outside, deciding to deposit his money in the bank. As he walked down the street, a red, two - door El Dorado rolled slowly down the street and stopped in front of his house. He watched as Cambria came running out of the front door to meet her visitor. Devontae walked back toward the house and arrived just as she finished planting a passionate kiss on the lips of a man, who was at least twenty years old.

‘Who the fuck is this nigga?’ Devontae asked, outraged by the scene.

‘Don’t be rude, this is my boyfriend, Red.’

‘Oh, so that’s supposed to be cute cause he got a car that’s Red too? Man, get the fuck out o’ here.’

‘Who is this lil’ nigga trynna front? Do he know who I am? Cambria, you need to check this little punk before I handle him,’ said Red.

‘Devontae go somewhere, you don’t have no place in grown folks business,’ Cambria said desperately.

‘Grown folks! Cambria, what the fuck? You only sixteen. Think about it, why would a nigga this grown want to talk to you? Cause you’re young and naïve! Tell him to leave right now.’ Devontae stared at his sister pleadingly, hoping that she would come to her senses. He tried to keep his eyes focused on her but couldn’t help but to notice Red flexing his muscles and clenching his fists and most importantly the nine millimeter tucked carefully into his FUBU pants.

‘No, Devontae. You are naïve. Where do you think I get the money from that I loan to you all the time. This man is responsible for the cloths on our backs. You should be thanking him.’ Red nodded in agreement.

Disgusted, Devontae spat on the ground and walked away. ‘Mannnn, fuck him! And his money!’

‘Your little brother got some balls. I like little niggas wit’ heart but I’ll whoop his little skinny ass next time he disrespects me. You know that right?’

‘Yeah, I know. Please don’t hurt him tho bae, he didn’t mean any harm,’ Cambria pleaded as she caressed his face.

Devontae was in a state of delirium but he was unsure how to blow off the steam. So angry that it was painful to move. He felt his feet, stomach, finger tips, and even ears burning, sizzling with rage. A quick escape route was what he needed, somewhere to just clear his mind. A destination far, far away but he wasn’t sure where to go or how to get there. One thing he knew for sure was how to get to the bank, so he continued walking without looking back at his sister and her so called ‘boyfriend.’ Down the street he could see Kristin Reese waiting for him at the corner. She was a pretty, yet peculiar girl but most importantly, she was a timely distraction.

Kristin walked with him to the bank and then to the library. Sitting quietly as he read through books about gambling and the art of mastering various games including black jack, poker and craps. He encouraged her to find a book to read but she wasn’t interested. So she waited, picking at her finger nail polish and biting her nails, glancing around suspiciously every once in a while but never so much as moved toward a bookshelf. Her conversations were mundane. She liked to talk about his hair, his eyes and nose, pretty much anything that would flatter him. She also talked about her favorite movie stars, music artists, female sports players, and cartoon characters. He compared everything she said to Nawiri’s conversations, who liked to go on and on about the books they read in English, and to share random facts about health, sports and world events. He was glad when they arrived at her house because the boredom was starting to show in his face though it had been a nice break from the days' arguments and confrontations. Before she got to the door, he grabbed her wrist and she looked at him knowingly. She followed him back to his house where she let him take out his frustrations on her body. He told her to meet him after school the next day, so that they could 'talk' more. She agreed without hesitation.

IF I AIN'T GOT YOU

The next day, Devontae ate with the athletes. He was becoming quite the popular kid with his street cred, charisma, dimples, finger waves and his new found knack for football. Those attributes were really the only criteria necessary for a boy to be popular. Nawiri was disgusted by his behavior the previous day, so she avoided eye contact with him. Their forced nonchalant attitudes made class extremely uncomfortable for both of them. Even Mr. Edison noticed that neither of them was answering the pre-algebra questions that he posed to the class and that their gazes seemed to focus on objects in opposite directions of the room. Sasha was stuck between the two of them, trying to keep the peace. When she found her efforts to be useless, she resulted to just being Nawiri's friend for the day, since it made her life easier and Devontae didn't seem to care either way.

'Girl, don't even bother with being mad at him. He is so immature that he can't help himself. You need to date an older guy that knows how to treat a girl right,' said Sasha reassuringly.

'Yeah, maybe. I mean this whole thing is so strange because we really are just friends. I don't know why we're acting this way toward each other. I shouldn't even care what he thinks about me and what does he care what I do, like if I decide to pay for your skates? I'm so confused,' said Nawiri.

She was so perplexed that she decided to make another attempt to speak to him after school, mustering up the courage to catch up to him as he made his way toward the front doors. But to her dismay, he told her not to walk too close to him as to not make his new 'girl' mad and then proceeded to meet a random chick, whom Nawiri had never seen before, at the entrance of the school. She was a caramel complexion, with Shirley temple curls and a plaid mini-skirt, which gave away the fact that she did not attend Century Academy because their uniform was white and navy blue. She was sucking on a 25¢ lollipop. 'Humph. So this is the kind of girl he wants? O.K. To hell with this nigga,' Nawiri thought. She sucked her teeth and walked away quickly before tear drops could form in her eyes. She wiped them clear before reaching her mom's car and silently swore revenge.

A week later, Nawiri and Sasha were in the midst of some of the most artistic boys at Century. They were the ones who rapped all day and practiced their instruments all night. Andrew, the finest one of the group, had his arm around Nawiri's shoulder as he shared some of his rap lyrics with her, to impress the girl for whom the song was written. It was entitled, 'Chocolate Beauty.' She'd never cared to mingle with many Century boys but her recent interactions had revealed to her that there were many boys who had secret crushes on her but were too intimidated to show how they felt.

As she reached in her backpack for a pencil to write a chorus to his song, she felt a sharp tug on her right arm. Turning around, she found Devontae standing behind her with a look of fury in his eyes. Andrew turned around as well.

'Hey, what's up Devontae? I hear you got mad flow man, you should come kick it with us sometime. So we can collaborate, you know what I'm sayin'? Maybe even record some stuff,' said Andrew with excitement.

'Yeah, maybe dawg. But first, I wanna know why you got your arm around Nawiri, like she's your girl?'

Andrew removed his arm slowly. 'I mean, she's cool, we were just hanging out. I don't want any problems man.'

Nobody at Century wanted to be a part of any altercation with Devontae. They had never seen him fight but his bullet wounds made him a walking reminder of the violence that existed around them. 'Nawiri can I talk to you for a minute?' Devontae asked more gently.

Nawiri was in shock and also scared of what he might do, she had never seen such a furious look in his eyes. 'Only if you wipe that crazy look off your face,' she said in a concerned voice.

'I'm not going to hurt you, dang, I would hope you know me better than that! I just want to talk if that's o.k. with you,' he said in an even softer tone. Nawiri looked at him in disbelief. 'So now he wants to talk after that shit he pulled last week? I can't believe this nigga. NO, I don't know who you are actually and clearly you don't know me either. Ok, pull it together Nawiri. Say yes or no, it's that simple. Hurry up and make a decision.' Everyone else stood quietly as Nawiri struggled with her internal conflict between pride and love.

She agreed reluctantly and they headed down the hallway. All of the artistic boys and Sasha watched them retreat into the school library and then tried to continue their conversation, attempting to ignore the strange occurrence and to shake off the eeriness that had swept the corridor.

The library was like a magical place for Devontae, where different worlds came alive and took hold of his consciousness. He had developed a bond with the librarian, Mr. Osborn, who frequently suggested books to Devontae that he thought might be of interest to him. Devontae would read in the morning before the start of school and sometimes between classes during the ten minute passing periods. Mr. Osborn had never seen a child with such a dedication to books, so it wasn't a surprise when he entered the library with the girl who consumed the other half of his thoughts. He led her to the library rear, to a secluded table surround by tall, overflowing bookshelves. They sat and he took her hand in his.

The intense gaze between them was electrifying and terrifying at the same time. There was no turning back and no turning away. After a few minutes, he pulled his chair closer to hers, holding her hand steadily and speaking slowly and softly, 'Nawiri, you are the most beautiful girl I have ever laid eyes on. Your intelligence is like fire to my spirit. You make it worth waking up at six'o clock every morning, so that I can come to school and be blessed by your presence. Before you, I was lost. I had no friends, no self-confidence and very little hope for the future. But now, even the thought of you inspires me to be better every day. To learn more, to know more, to acquire more, and to be a better man. I know we're young and maybe I'm being a little over the top but I don't think it's every day that a fourteen year old realizes what a jewel they have in their life. If you can just find it in your heart to forgive me for my petty games, to forgive me for hurting your feelings and for being rude, for being hypersensitive about money issues and just for being an asshole in general. You don't deserve to be around anyone negative and I don't want to be that person. Will you forgive me?'

Perhaps it was too much intensity because she tried to respond but her mouth was frozen shut. So, Devontae waited patiently for her to process his speech and to formulate a coherent response. A few minutes later, she came to and found her voice again. 'What happened?' she asked, bewildered. 'I think you zoned out for a second. Maybe I admitted too much,' Devontae laughed. She looked at him with the most serious face and responded, 'It was not too much,' and kissed him lightly on the cheek. Devontae felt a tingle down his spine, an ecstasy of sorts. His hands began to sweat and Nawiri laughed, 'Ugh, your hands are sticky. Are you nervous to be around me or somethin'?' she teased.

'No, not at all. Actually, I feel like life is exactly the way it should be, when I'm around you,' he said and moved quickly to kiss her on the lips, placing his hand behind the nape of her neck. Nawiri was stunned, she felt like one of those cartoon characters after they'd run into a wall and had many stars circling around their forehead.

'So, what does this mean?' she asked, sincerely, 'Do we go together now?'

'Honestly, I don't think I'm ready for that with you. I think if we decide to be together, it should be later on, maybe in high school. Right now, I'm not ready to be your boyfriend. I don't think I can offer you what you deserve,' he said with sad eyes.

'Well, what exactly is it that I deserve? You think I want you to buy me things? I know you don't have a job, why would I expect that from you?'

'You don't understand. I'm not mentally or emotionally ready to give you the support and love that a girl like you should get from her man. But I can promise, for sure, that I will be a better friend from now on.'

Nawiri was disappointed; she didn't understand the use of telling her how he felt if he didn't want them to be a couple. Perhaps it was these types of strange ideas and perspectives that kept her intrigued by him.

They left the library walking to a new rhythm, both sensing that a new chapter of their lives together was beginning. They discussed summer plans, deciding that it was absolutely necessary that they see one another over the three month break. Nawiri had a three week summer camp to attend but she promised to visit him when she got back in town. To solidify the deal, they devised a plan to tell their parents they were working on a science project, when they were really going to be using one of her grandmother's nutrition programs for autistic children and implementing it with his younger sister, Tanisha. Sasha was also a part of the plans though Nawiri would need to ask her later if she was down. She assumed that she would be with nothing much else to do but find boys around Conner Creek. One endeavor Nawiri could never quite understand.

Sometimes she wondered how people so confusing to her could be her best friends but always came to the conclusion that underneath the superficial layers, they all wanted the same things – love, peace of mind, and happiness. Sasha seemed to be most concerned with love; Devontae with peace of mind; and Nawiri was pursuing happiness in all shapes and forms.

GONE TIL NOVEMBER

Summer was off to an adventurous start. G'Ma and Nawiri drove for miles and miles up through the woodlands of Michigan to reach Camp Nautical. There was actually much more land there than water but the camp director had chosen the name to emphasize the beautiful lake that they used for sailing, tubing, water skiing, canoeing, kayaking, swimming, and row boating. The sun was just reaching its noon high as they approached the entrance gates. The chrome plated steel bars towered over them, with a fancy curvature at the top and decorative posts. It felt as if they were entering into the gardens of a remote castle. The gate operator pushed a button and the gate opened electronically, allowing them to drive onto the gravel road leading to the main office for registration.

G'Ma felt like she was back home in Georgia. She had missed the comfort of the trees, the still freshness of the country air and the humming noises made by the small creatures of the land. Memories surfaced as she recalled the times when she and her younger brother Ronny had gone to the river to catch fish for dinner. Ronny had always been the better fisherman, so he coached her until she became a master at the craft. She could see Betty Mae, Anna Reese, and Ernett Witherspoon running down the street to meet her, so that they could go play in Ms. Jensen's huge backyard. They always teased Betty for wearing boys' baseball caps. And she would respond defiantly, 'My momma says that it will protect me from being burnt by the sun! Now ya'll will be sorry once you get your forehead burned and then, you will be envying me.' And sure enough, she was right. 'Those were the days,' thought G'Ma as she parked her Mercedes carefully next to a burgundy Range Rover.

'G'Ma! G'Ma! G'Ma! Snap out of it, I've been calling your name for the past ten minutes and you are just daydreaming and driving like you can't hear me!' Nawiri was amazed that her grandmother could tune out the sound of her voice so well. 'What do you want child? I was just reminiscing on the old days. All of this greenery takes me back to life in Georgia.'

''Oh, well, I didn't really want much. I only wanted to ask you how much this camp costs.'

G'Ma puckered her lips, 'Mmm, you are steady asking about how much something costs. Why can't you just enjoy the experience and let me and your mother worry about the expense? Sometimes, you can be just a little too inquisitive. It is $7,500 for the three weeks. Now don't ask me no more questions.'

Nawiri was shocked. She didn't know for sure but suspected that $7,500 was a lot of money for a summer camp. After registration, G'Ma drove away still dazzled by the outdoors, planning her next visit to Georgia. Nawiri was lonely for all of five minutes before her animated camp counselor stepped into the cabin, 'Hellooooooo! How are you doing today?!! Are you ready for a summer of fun and excitement?!!' Before Nawiri could answer, she was already explaining the activities for the day, 'Today, we'll just be chilling out, you know? Within the hour, most of your cabin mates should be here, then we'll all head over to the dining hall together to eat an awesome, nutritious meal. And then the kick-off camp fire is tonight! You'll LOVE that, it is absolutely fabulous. And yeah dude, that's about it. No sneaking boys in here and we'll be good all summer! Here are some materials to make a name tag for your bed and I'll be back in a few!' She left as quickly as she came, leaving Nawiri baffled by her fast paced accent.

One by one, the other girls came into the cabin. There was Kate from Bloomfield Hills, Shelly from Muskegon, Kristie from the Upper Peninsula, Mary from Ann Arbor, Natalie from Chicago, Melanie from Wisconsin, Stephanie from Grosse Pointe, and Helen from Farmington Hills. No one could pronounce Nawiri's name correctly, so they settled on NaDee, which stood for Nawiri from Detroit. She didn't really like it but decided it wasn't worth making a fuss over. The girls seemed to clique up fast. They spoke about their pet horses and vacation homes, some bonded over playing the same instrument or having the same favorite television show, movies and bands. Nawiri felt awkward, she barely watched television, had no pets, no siblings, no vacation homes, no nanny, no video games, and no one played her instrument. She was also having a hard time keeping up with the pace of the conversations as everyone seemed to be talking over each other.

'I love to go rock climbing with my dad, we go every summer!'

‘That is so cool, I love hiking with my Dad at our cabin!’

‘Oh my gosh, have you guys ever been to the Poconos in Pennsylvania? They are so beautiful, I go every year with my whole family!’

‘O yeah, I’ve been there twice.’

‘I’ve only been once. But I have been to Hawaii three times. The water is so blue there and sparkles like crystals.’

‘O wow, my favorite color is blue.’

‘No way! So is mine!’

The conversations continued this way throughout dinner. Nawiri had the urge to jump into one of their conversations many times but it seemed there was very little opportunity to do so. She also wasn’t used to bragging about herself so much and couldn’t think of anything fast enough. By the time she came up with a line, they had already moved on to the next thing they’d done or seen or place they’d been to. No one really inquired about the other’s experiences; they only talked about their own. It was a very strange site indeed. When she spotted another black girl at the camp fire, she went over to sit next to her.

‘Hey, my name is Nawiri. What’s yours?’ The girl looked at her and smiled. She smiled back with a sigh of relief. They didn’t know one another but it seemed they had found familiarity in a strange place. ‘Hi Nawiri, my name is Destiny.’

'Destiny, I like that name, it sounds so magical,' lamented Nawiri.

'Thank you and I like your name, it sounds African,' Destiny replied.

'Well, it is. My parents wanted me to feel more connected to my roots I suppose. But that's definitely not gonna happen this summer,' she laughed.

'Girl, hecky naw. Not at this camp. So where are you from?'

'I'm from Detroit. You?'

'I'm from Flint but I got cousins in Detroit though. You know a girl named Nira Green?'

'Yes! She goes to Hally, right?'

They continued talking until the camp songs began. Nawiri was happy to have found a friend who she could relate to on a more personal level. The white girls just seemed to come from another planet. The way they communicated with one another was so foreign to her that she felt very uncomfortable and was ready to go home.

The bells sounded early in the morning and the girls dragged themselves out of bed. Their schedule was packed with activities. Breakfast, tie-dye shirt-making, swimming, lunch, kayaking, free time, dinner, camp fire, bedtime. Some kids opted to join the camp orchestra, so that they could practice their instruments, others took writing, acting, and craft workshops. Nawiri, Destiny and Melanie from Wisconsin made similar schedules, so that they could stick together. After the first week, Nawiri was more acclimated to her environment. Most girls in her cabin still weren't very approachable but those who were, allowed her to put cornrows and twisties in their hair. With all the time she spent doing hair, she considered charging especially since they took out her hard work so quickly, complaining about the pulling on their scalps. 'Don't ask me to do your hair if you're just going to take it out tomorrow!' Nawiri would fuss.

One day, she walked into the recital hall and was surprised to see it empty. A gleaming grand piano sat on the stage, black and glimmering in the dim stage light. She walked toward it, yearning to play a song that would embody all of her bottled up emotions. Sitting down, the first song that came to mind was 'A Song for Mama' by Boyz II Men. She began to play the harmony, while singing the chorus. She began to cry as she thought about how much she missed the mom she had before she became so cold and distant. She loved her grandmother dearly but no one could replace the love of her parents. And it was a love that she yearned for more than anything else. She heard footsteps in the hallway and ran to the back of the stage, exiting through the back door. Music had a way of pulling her emotions out, forcing her to shed tears that were long overdue. She wiped her face clean and headed back to the cabins to join the other girls for dinner.

Nawiri and her new friends Destiny and Melanie enjoyed Camp Nautical. The workshops were informative, the water was cool and refreshing, and the forest was scary at night but fun to hike through during the day. Discussing their experience, Destiny admitted, 'I really did not think I was going to have fun this summer. I'm so glad I met you guys. And Melanie, you are the coolest white girl I've ever met. Way more down to earth than these other girls.' Melanie blushed, 'And you are the coolest black girls I've ever met,' they laughed. One thing they all agreed on was that most of the kids there were arrogant and thought they knew everything. And for this reason, Nawiri couldn't wait to get home.

When Ms. Robyn came to pick her up, she was so happy that her daughter was speaking more proper English. 'Thank God! I need to send you to camp every summer because your little ghetto friends have been rubbing off on the way you talk.' Nawiri rolled her eyes at her mother, she couldn't wait to get home to see her, 'little ghetto friends.'

GET IT TOGETHER

They pulled into the main entrance of the complex. The 'Brightmoor Projects' was what they called it. Similar to a shanty town but with aluminum siding instead of plywood and flat roofs instead of tilted tin slate. Heaps of toys, strollers, and random car parts could be seen in some backyards. Weeds had been a pervasive issue in Brightmoor, so the complex manager kept the grass low, so low that most patches of grass appeared to be top soil.

Nawiri was fascinated. She lived only fifteen minutes away but had never been here before. On her street the lawns were full and neatly manicured, the homes were brick, decorated with vines and stained glass windows. But this street was much different. Children sat on the porches watching the silver Mercedes coup make its way slowly down the street. Ms. Heath was quiet, then spoke with a soft power that filled the vehicle. 'Now you know Nawiri, you must not eva judge a person who has less than you do. 'Cause believe it or not, I grew up even more poor than these children on this block. But we were never poor in spirit. We had so much energy and so much to be grateful for. I'm glad that even at this young age, you have chosen to have friends that are filled with the spirit of God. Money could never replace that.' Ms. Robyn rolled her eyes, silently disagreeing with her mother. She was, in fact, quite disgusted and was ready to turn the car around and go home.

They pulled up to Devontae's complex. Sasha and her mother were getting out of their jeep and Nawiri jumped out of the Mercedes and ran to greet them. On the front steps sat Momma Kiesha. She held onto the stair rail to support her weak and petite frame as she stood to greet the strangers who had arrived at her home. Eyeing them suspiciously, she called out to Cambria.

'What, Ma!'

'Come out here, who are these people you done invited over my house without tellin' me?'

Cambria's face appeared behind the screen door. 'I'on know them!'

'Devontae!!'

He was already at the door. 'Sorry, Momma. These are my guests, we're gonna do some studying and work on a school project. I told Cambria.' He paused and then whispered, 'I guess I just forgot to tell you.'

'Mmhmm,' she turned to Ms. Heath and Ms. Karena. Devontae slid off of the porch and joined Nawiri and Sasha on the sidewalk. They were each holding their breath in anticipation of the ensuing conversation between their mothers.

'Well, hello' Keisha greeted the other mothers, her head swaying and lips pressed, sizing them up 'I see ya'll rolling through my neighborhood wit'cha fancy cars and shit. So you judging me? That's what you doing right? Yeah, I already know.'

Devontae yelled out instinctively, 'Momma, stop!!'

'Shut up boy!'

'Look I don't even know you, I don't have time for no mess. You up here actin' all ghetto for no reason. Calm your ass down,' replied Ms. Karena.

'O so now I'm ghetto?! Bitch, I'll…'

'Wait…wait…wait… I think we are getting off on the wrong foot. Hello, my name is Annett Heath and this here is my granddaughter, Nawiri Simmons. Now, I can see that you were not prepared for visitors, so we are more than willing to take the children back to our house.' Ms. Robyn added, 'I believe there will be more space for them to do their work anyway,' she said peering into the living room. 'I can see it is quite a mess in there.'

'How dare you insult my home! I don't want to know yo' name, I want to know why you on my front porch wit' your little goody-two-shoes daughters, that one look like she blind with them big'ol glasses,' she said, pointing at Nawiri. Keisha's dark eyes squinted with furry as she prepared to launch her verbal attack.

'Hold on! Don't be comin' at her daughter, who are you? Rude Heffa, say some more insulting shit and I'll knock you into next week! You betta watch yo mothafuckin' mouth!'

‘I dare you to hit me!’

‘No, there won’t be any fighting today!’ Ms. Heath proclaimed.

‘Who the hell are you? You ain’t nobody’s Momma! You rich hoes always trynna control somebody.’

‘Say one more thing about her or her daughter and I swear to God I’ma kick your ass,’ yelled Ms. Karena.

‘And who made you her guardian? If she wanna fight me, let her fight.’

‘Whoa, I don’t want any parts of a fight, I only want to allow them to spend some time together for a few hours. Why are you being so difficult?’ asked Ms. Robyn.

‘Cause you don’t belong here!’

‘Says who? Just because I’m not poor, I can’t come to the hood?’ asked Ms. Robyn.

‘So, you callin’ me poor? You don’t know what I got! You uppity bitch!’

‘Call me bitch again and I’ll show you what bitch really means!’ Ms. Robyn snapped.

‘I dare you!’

Now the three of them were going off at the same time. No more space was left for listening; only a constant stream of yelling, finger pointing, neck rolling and insults, which escalated such that the children could only hear the sound of indiscrete bickering and high-pitched screeches as Keisha's voice reached the height of its limited range. As the arguing continued, Ms. Heath grew tired of the pointless insults and slipped away beckoning for Nawiri to leave with her. Nawiri stood still, frozen. Partly from the shock of the argument but mostly because she did not want to leave. She wanted to stay with her friends to work on the project they had been planning for months. The project that she had obsessed over and had waited patiently to start. 'Now, is our chance,' she thought, 'I can't just leave!'

As Ms. Heath walked forward to grab her, Nawiri turned abruptly and started to run as fast as she could. Sasha immediately turned and ran after her. Then, Devontae turned heel and toe racing after the both of them, to bring them back. Ms. Heath tried to catch them but her aching hip restricted her pace and Keisha tried as well but her heart was too weak. Ms. Robyn and Ms. Karena stood on the porch watching all of them run out of the complex and into the city. They shook their heads, walked to their vehicles and drove away. 'Whatever, she'll come home eventually and if not, whatever,' Ms. Karena thought and Ms. Robyn was running late for a business meeting.

Nawiri, Sasha, and Devontae ran until they had lost their mothers and when they finally stopped, Devontae did not attempt to drag them back to the house. Instead, he sat down on the grass to reflect on what had just occurred. He hadn't been running after them after all, he was in fact running away as well. The park was empty except for a few kids on the basketball court. Sasha walked in circles with her hands covering her face, they could hear the muffled sound of weeping. Nawiri stood, staring at her feet. She was embarrassed by her mother's words. The ignorance, the intolerance, the lack of understanding, and the inability of these grown women to have a simple conversation with one another. They were all embarrassed. Devontae wished he could rewind the last ten minutes of his life back to a time when his friends did not know this part of his life, when he didn't have to be ashamed because it was all a secret. The weeping willow whose trunk Devontae was seated on, cast a shadow over their small frames offering relief from the relentless sun. Nawiri spoke, suddenly, afraid that too much silence would somehow destroy their connection to one another. 'So, maybe we can just start the project here at the park.'

'Or maybe we can't.' Devontae replied bluntly. Nawiri went quiet again. 'We're not our parents, you know? We don't have to make the same mistakes; we don't have to be closed–minded and insensitive. I think we're different. We still have…'

'We still have what?!' Sasha retorted through streaming hot tears. 'I don't have shit. Nawiri, you got everything, why don't you give me some! Nobody loves me, nobody wants me. My momma would rather defend you than defend me, her *own* daughter!'

Devontae looked up at Sasha; he had never heard her yell or even cry, as she was always laughing at his or Nawiri's jokes. 'Sasha, you see where I live? You see my momma? She's a crack head! You know the ones that everybody at school always talk about? Every stupid thing that somebody does, somebody else says, 'Maannnnn, you a crack head!' You want to talk about having nothing! You see that uniform I wear to school? I wash that every night cause it's the only uniform shirt and pants I got!' His voice was cracking with anger and his arms were swinging with animation as he balanced himself on his knees. 'So, don't tell me about not having anything.'

They sat quietly, not knowing where to go or what to say. No one wanted to offend another; they had all been offended enough for one day. Their entire lives were flashing before their eyes as they evaluated themselves and their sense of self-worth. At school, they seemed to be identical in nature but their mothers had revealed one painful difference – money. It was a factor in their lives that they couldn't control and yet it seemed to dictate the actions of everyone around them including their own parents. Divided and weak, the blissful chapter of ignorance was over as the truth seeped into their shared reality.

'Her ghetto ass. Why did she have to be home today? Sitting on the front porch of all places. Not in the kitchen, not in the living room. Just posted on the damn porch wit' nothin' else to do but terrorize people. I ain't never seen her act out like that. Fuckin' drugs man. They destroying her personality too. Nawiri probably don't wanna have shit to do wit' me. Momma fucked everything up!' Devontae glanced over at the other two, just to make sure they couldn't tell what he was thinking but they seemed to be entranced in their own thoughts.

Sasha was lying on her side with her head resting in the palm of her hand. 'It's cool. That's fine. Don't stand up for me. Thought I didn't see you pull off without trying to get me back. I saw your bitch ass. What kind of mother just doesn't give a damn about her own child? Why did she even have me? At least she's not as ghetto as Devontae's momma. Damn. To hell with all this drama, I'm goin' to see Anthony tonight. Suga Daddy numba three.' Sasha chuckled to herself and caught eyes with Nawiri who was also entranced with internal dialogue, 'I just don't understand why she has to be so elitist. She thought I didn't notice how scared she looked but I saw. And then calling Devontae's place junky and calling their family poor. Wow. Mom, you got a lot of nerve. And to be so foul in front of her own mother!'

A blind, elderly man was passing by with his guide dog and stopped on the sidewalk as he approached them. 'Why, you kids look disastrous. You should be playing and enjoying this beautiful day!' he suggested, brightly.

Devontae was not in the mood for advice, 'You should be minding your own business,' he retorted.

'Hmm, it is interesting, the concept of business,' the old man said, chuckling.

Nawiri chimed in, trying to make up for Devontae's attitude, 'I have a question for you!'

'Sure! Ask away,' said the man.

'If you could give one piece of advice about living; about how to really live a full and happy life. What would you say?'

'Well, I would have to say two things, first you gotta *Love* and then you gotta *Respect* yourself and your neighbors. Your neighbor could be the person who sleeps in the room next to you, it could be the person down the street, it could even be this lovely willow tree towering over you. All living things deserve love and respect, even you. And of course giving to yourself is easy but if you don't know yourself, well then it's harder to give yourself love and respect. It should be the natural way of life, you know? But often we forget these things. And there are always consequences to forgetting. Anyway, I must get going. I hope you don't waste the rest of the day staring at the ground, be careful or the dust might just wisp you away.'

The children reflected on his words. Then, Sasha thought of another question, 'What if your neighbor doesn't love you back?!' She jumped up and ran around the large pine tree that was blocking her view from the direction that the old man had walked in but when she got around the tree, he was nowhere in sight. She came back and sat down, disappointed.

'So, what did he say?' Nawiri asked.

'He was gone!'

'Did you notice?' said Devontae.

'Notice what?' Nawiri and Sasha chorused together.

'He was blind.'

'Yeah, so what?' replied Sasha.

'But he saw us and he saw the Willow tree.'

They sat in silence, not knowing how to explain his strange appearance, sense of sight, and disappearance behind the trees. In the spirit of wisdom, understanding and the magical aura left behind by the blind man who could see, Nawiri expressed a new idea. It was a long stretch, something foreign, abstract, perhaps even absurd. But they needed a solution, something to save their young, negative thought-ridden minds and to save their friendship. She couldn't tell Sasha and Devontae how to deal with their respective situations. Who was she to do so? A rich kid with a supportive, loving grandmother. It was a wonder they could stand being around her. Even though they had no idea how much she missed the presence of her mother and father in her life.

She spoke slowly and firmly, attempting to chide the ice between them with the dullest pick in her friendship tool bag. The idea was simple; they would sit in a circle – triangle in this case – with backs straight, legs crossed, arms relaxed, eyes closed. Sasha and Devontae were skeptical at first, resistant but not militant, which was a relief to Nawiri. The next part would seem like the easiest but in fact it was the hardest. The key to this mystery idea of 'meditation' was the mind and the breath. Clearing their minds and focusing on breathing, counting, and listening to their environment all at the same time. Each of them found themselves drifting into habitual thoughts and quickly shifting back to counting, imagining blank space like a canvas where only they could create, erase and start all over again. After thirty minutes, someone coughed and startled the other two. With eyes open, they seemed to be in a daze, quiet observers of a world different from the one that had existed before they closed their eyes.

‘Let’s go back!’ said Devontae with newfound enthusiasm, ‘We need to start making Tanisha’s meals.’

HEADED IN THE RIGHT DIRECTION

They were surprised to see Ms. Heath and Momma Kiesha sitting on the porch together in what seemed like deep conversation. After the kids had taken off, they had walked back to the front porch and sat panting as they tried to catch their breath. Ms. Robyn and Ms. Karena were long gone. Their breathing slowly came back to normal and they caught one another's eyes, triggering something inside of them. Bursting into hysterical and pitiful laughter. Painful and suffocating gasps for air between cackles. Tears streaming from the energy spent and the loss of control. They laughed to clear the air, to erase the embarrassment, to hide the battle wounds and to mend the invisible link that had already been severed within the first two minutes of meeting one another. It was a deep laugh filled with emotion, sucking in the water vapor from the air and returning sadness, grief, and regret. They laughed because it hurt to have their children run away from them and even more because the children had been right. Then, there was silence. The eye catching was over because each set of eyes was cast to the ground in shame. Kiesha realized that it was her turn to be the bigger person, since she had sparked the entire situation, 'I'm so sorry for what I said,' she paused, letting her apology resonate and linger in the air before she continued, 'I'm embarrassed. I had no right. You didn't deserve it. I'm just weak. I look at my children and I envy them for their strength. They hate me and what I do, the person I've become. Especially Devontae, he looks at me with those eyes. He doesn't need to say it, his eyes tell me everything.'

Ms. Heath had not expected for Kiesha to open up so quickly after such an appalling greeting but she realized then, that there was much more to the emotional explosion than what she had witnessed on the surface. 'Darling, you are not beholden to the things that Devontae hates. I can assure you that if he even hates anything at all, it surely isn't you. Perhaps he doesn't like something that you say or consistently do, well it never hurts to ask and then you can figure out if it's something you're willing to change. It's never too late; every moment is a window of opportunity for change.'

'But you don't understand, I can't change.'

'As far as I'm concerned, can't is not even a word. You can do anything you put your mind to.'

'You don't understand. Nobody understands. I just can't. It's not in my power.'

'These are mental boundaries that you have created. No one or nothing can take away your ability to self-reflect and improve. You hold the lock and key. How old are you honey?'

'Thirty,' replied Kiesha softly.

Ms. Heath straightened her back, struggling to repress the look of shock that was creeping onto her face. Telling wrinkles of fifty years had begun to settle along the creases of Kiesha's eyes. The drugs had hardened her skin and the bags under her eyes were dark and hung low. Her beauty could not be erased but her age was completely indiscernible to a stranger like Ms. Heath.

Ms. Heath cleared her throat, 'Well, then you have even more reason to be hopeful. You have at least fifty more years ahead of you to become the person you want to be. Darling, I am seventy five years old and I've got at least another thirty years in this old body. You can be my new walking partner,' she smiled.

When the children walked up cautiously, three hours later, it was this conversation that had consumed these women. So much that they did not even look surprised to see the kids.

'Mmhmm, I knew you all would come back sooner or later. After you left, we realized how silly the whole thing was and began to talk. The time slipped by so quickly, I even forgot to call the police. You all are lucky. Anyhow, Nawiri, you have about another hour, so if you want to make some progress with this project you'd better start now because your mother is coming back to pick us up!' Ms. Heath said firmly. Momma Kiesha added an, 'I'm sorry Devontae,' but he ignored her. Ms. Heath and Momma Kiesha continued talking as the three children entered the house. Anisha and Tanisha were in front of the television set, as usual. But today they were holding brand new Barbie dolls that Red had bought them for their birthday.

Tanisha began to make strange noises and she appeared to be very agitated, shaking her head back and forth. Devontae knew that it was because of the unexpected visitors. 'Girls,' he said firmly, 'These are my friends – Nawiri and Sasha. You're going to be seeing a lot more of them because they are helping me with a project.'

Tanisha was still rocking and shaking her head in a vehement protest against his visitors. He motioned for them to proceed to the kitchen as he stayed behind to contain the situation.

'See now, you went and made her upset,' accused Anisha.

'Be quiet, where are those books I bought you for your birthday?'

'I don't know. Upstairs somewhere.'

'Well, you need to find them because tonight we're gonna sit down and read through one of them.'

'Aww, man,' Anisha replied with a look of devastation.

Tanisha was accustomed to this type of conversation between Anisha and Devontae, which seemed to calm her nerves. He gave them each a warm hug, told them that he loved them and then joined Nawiri and Sasha in the kitchen.

'Why doesn't your sister like us?' asked Nawiri, whose feelings were slightly hurt.

'It's not that she doesn't like you. She's just not used to you, so you threw her off a little, she's fine.'

‘Oh ok, I guess,’ Nawiri replied, not completely convinced as she pulled the nutrition meal plan for autistic children out of her bag. The recipes were based on a Gluten Free and Casein Free (GFCF) diet. Devontae had already purchased the required products; it was the longest grocery list he had ever seen. Eggs, broccoli, corn, green beans, orange juice, peas, spinach, chicken breast, turkey, peaches, pears, baked beans, GFCF bread, tomatoes, corn tortillas, GFCF cornbread mix, Corn Flakes, Rice Chex cereal, black beans, navy beans, pinto beans, grits, jelly, rice milk, canola oil, GFCF pancake mix, GFSF pasta, peanut butter, maple syrup, rice, salad dressing, apples, bananas, green bell peppers, carrots, celery, eggplant, garlic cloves, green onion, mushrooms, onion, oranges, potatoes, lettuce, tomatoes, brown sugar, chili powder, cinnamon, ground cumin, oregano leaves, real vanilla extract and thyme leaves. They split up tasks and began to make Tanisha’s meals for the week. Devontae was in charge of breakfast, Nawiri was in charge of lunch and Sasha was handling dinner because she had the most experience with cooking. The kitchen was full of mouth-watering aromas with rice cooking on the stove, chicken breast seasoned with chili powder in the oven and vegetable stir fry sizzling in the largest skillet they could find on the stove.

Following her nose, Cambria entered the kitchen and stood in awe. ‘Wow! I can’t believe ya’ll in here throwin’ down like this. So, what’s the occasion?’

‘We’re creating a new meal plan for Tanisha,’ said Devontae.

‘What’s wrong with what she eats now?’

‘Cambria, you know she don’t digest the junk you feed her that well. Her stomach is always hurting. They say this new diet will even help with her communication skills.’

‘I guess,’ she opened the refrigerator, ‘Hold on! I know you did not spend all my food stamps on all this health freak food! Where is my damn card Devontae? I’m not playin’ wit’ you!’ Cambria yelled. She was already uncomfortable with all of the females crowding her space, with the two women on the porch and the two girls in the kitchen. But spending all of her grocery money was an infringement that would surely push her over the top.

‘Naw, there’s still like fifty dollars on there for this month. But listen, I got another hundred in cash for you, right here and you can eat this food, it’s not gonna kill you. I bought it to make these specific meals for Tanisha but there’s enough for all of us.’

‘Gimme that,’ Cambria snatched the money and went in the living room to watch television with the twins. Devontae shook his head and went back to pouring corn flakes into sandwich bags for Tanisha’s afternoon snacks.

The rest of the summer was like this. They would make the meals on Sundays, administer throughout the week and record behavioral observations and changes. Ms. Heath made a purpose of staying and chatting with Momma Kiesha whenever she was home and Kiesha stayed home on certain days, anticipating the visit. Even Ms. Karena and Ms. Robyn had begun to stick around instead of driving off in a hurry. They enjoyed talking with the other mothers and listening to Ms. Heath's aged wisdom; the conversations seemed to be chipping away at some of their sharp and jagged edges. To the children's disbelief, their mother's had actually become friends.

Sitting on the front porch made them feel like kids again, telling petty secrets and teasing one another for their shallow insecurities. They were especially amused when old heads, like Snappy, would walk by and comment on their overflowing beauty, give fake marriage proposals and shower compliments from their brilliant eyes to their well-manicured toes. They would usually respond by saying they were too old to be fooled by those types of lame pick-up lines but they were flattered none the less. Early evening – a few hours before sunset – was the perfect time for their chat. The breeze picked up and the offset sun directed most of its heat waves toward a different set of porches further west. Under the pleasant shade of the petite awning, silent moments were embraced with thoughtful reflection. Their energies were in sync and calm, radiating even in the presence of pests and mosquitoes. Walks through the neighborhood were a hotter option but more eventful and adventurous. Ms. Heath, Ms. Robyn and Ms. Karena missed the kind of free flowing interactions between neighbors from their childhoods that they observed in Brightmoor. Children were in and out of various homes; adults stood on front lawns talking to neighbors, swapping stories, secrets and recipes or arguing, sometimes even fighting. Refraining from talk of disappointing ex-husbands and ex-boyfriends, they preferred to speak of their secret crushes and spicy love affairs. Ms. Robyn, who was currently seeing a young stud, – ten years her junior – was completely mystified by his almond eyes and blissful skills in the sack. Momma Kiesha was falling for a neighbor of hers and Ms. Karena was still enjoying the single, celibate life. Ms. Heath knew she would never re-marry and was quite disturbed to hear that her daughter was dating yet couldn't take time out to spend with Nawiri.

'Robyn, let me talk to you for a second,' Ms. Heath pulled her daughter aside and took a deep breath. 'I've been patient and I've been soft,' Ms, Robyn tried to interrupt, 'Wait, let me finish. I have watched you fade away into the distance emotionally and physically for six years. Your interactions with your own daughter are deplorable. Right now, she basically has only one parent and it's not you. I refuse to continue to watch you neglect your child. Either I will take her back to Georgia with me or you can get your act together and start acting like a mother. Honey, I know that man hurt you. I know he was distant and cold. He never let you into his secret world and now you are doing the same thing to us. Now, is that fair? Nawiri never asked you to have her. She didn't ask to be brought into this world. Don't make her suffer because you are suffering. Replacing her with a secret boyfriend. I am boiling inside right now. How could you?'

Ms. Robyn began to cry, 'Momma, I'm so sorry. I just didn't know what to do.'

'Well what you've done is miss out on six years of motherhood. I'm not trying to make you feel guilty but at some point you have to hold up the mirror and face the truth. Don't be afraid to talk to me, to write out your feelings in a journal, to pray, to meditate, to share with these other beautiful women that we are with now, to cry, to sing, to laugh, and to put all that energy that you put into your work back into yourself as love. No man should ever be able to make you feel empty if your heart is already full of love and joy.'

Still crying, 'Momma, why didn't you have this talk with me before now?'

'Because I knew you weren't ready to receive the message,' Ms. Heath smiled. She wiped her daughter's tears. Ms. Robyn cried and cried, laying her head on her mother's broad shoulder. It was the first time she had cried in six years, since the day he left. The secret abyss of emotions was overflowing into her eyes. Regret stabbing her heart. Ms. Heath added after some time, 'Nawiri is young and I am old, we can both forgive you as long as you can forgive yourself. Let's rejoin the ladies.' They walked around the corner back to the house to find Momma Kiesha and Ms. Karena sitting on the steps once more.

'So, what is it you think their doing in there?' Kiesha asked, 'our kids are like some mad scientists! Sometimes, I catch Devontae up at like four o'clock in the morning reading books!'

'Girl, me too! But you know we gotta be thankful that they're sneaking to read books and not to do other things!' exclaimed Ms. Karena.

'Amen to that!' said Ms. Heath.

‘So what are you all’s favorite past times? I know this is gonna be good! I’ll start first, I love to garden and grow fresh vegetables like I used to do back home in Georgia!’

It didn’t take Ms. Karena much effort to think of hers, ‘Singing! I looovveee to sing! Not around anyone else, of course! But if you catch me off guard when I’m at home alone, nine times out of ten, I’ll be in the middle of a Michael Jackson song. Beat it, Beat it, Beat it, know I got to Beat It, Beat It!’

They all laughed.

‘How about you Kiesha? What do you love to do?’ asked Ms. Karena.

‘Me, I don’t know. Guess I never really thought about it. I, um,’ she started to twitch and scratch her arm.

‘It’s ok baby, it’s ok. You don’t have to know, it was just a silly question,’ said Ms. Heath with a warm, comforting voice.

Ms. Heath was very worried. She knew that Kiesha was struggling with some kind of addiction but hadn’t quite figured out what to say or if she should even say anything at all. After all, it was none of her business.

‘And Ms. Robyn, what is yours?’ Asked Ms. Karena again, everyone was eager to hear her response. ‘Well, momma, you don’t even know this one,’ she looked at Ms. Heath with a smile, ‘I have notebooks full of pencil sketches. I usually draw after work when I retreat to my room for hours sometimes. I can hear you and Nawiri talking downstairs and I draw where I envision you sitting and sometimes I draw the stories that she describes from school and I draw her smiling and happy. Even though I could go down to see her myself, I stay in my room and imagine, interpreting what I hear into pencil pictures.'

They were all in shock. Ms. Karena and Momma Keisha had no idea before now that she didn't have a close relationship with her daughter. And Ms. Heath had no idea that Robyn was still paying attention to her daughter from a far. Each of them reached out to her and touched some part of her body. Her hands, shoulder and face were covered with warm, open hands and then they surrounded her with a hug, an embrace that they all needed.

PRESSURE

Walking to the library, Devontae picked up a stick and hit it on the ground as he thought of new rap lyrics for a song he was writing with Junior. It was a slow day; Sasha and Nawiri never came on Wednesdays, so he had to find other things to keep himself occupied. The sun was ablaze; he could feel the sweat beads forming on his forehead. But the heat didn't stop the kids from playing. They were outside riding bikes and doing crazy flips through sprinklers. Some were barbequing at Young John and Thomas' house; his aunty, the same one who had opened the door the first night he went over there to shoot dice was on the porch balancing the biggest pork rib he had ever seen between her barbeque sauce drenched fingers. There was a stereo on the steps bumping 'Country Grammar' by Nelly and all John's girl cousins were clearly loving this song because they were dancing like they were in the music video itself. They rocked and twisted their hips, twirled in circles with their arms held up in the air and fingers snapping on the baseline. He watched until he caught Aunty staring at him from the porch. He turned away and continued on the sidewalk, enduring the summer heat waves.

He was almost to the library when a game on the basketball court caught his eye. Basketball wasn't really his thing but the game looked intense, so he stepped inside the gate, to watch for a few minutes and ask for the score. He was familiar with some of the guys on the court, their ages ranged from fourteen to seventeen. A few of them were in the local gang, they were involved in most of the store robberies and stick ups you heard about in those days. Devontae was never afraid; the only thing that scared him was failure. 'Ya'll niggas lookin' tired!' he laughed, 'this heat ain't no joke.' They agreed and went back to focusing on the game. The other guys on the side of the court were preparing for the next game; deciding who would go in and who would stay out.

'Aye Devontae, you wanna play dawg?'

'Naw, I'm good man. If ya'll seen my game, you would understand,' he laughed earnestly.

'Aight man, that's cool. I heard yo' crap game straight tho. But you ain't fuckin' wit' mine.'

'Probably not dawg. I'm on to some new shit anyway.'

The guys from the court finished their game and walked over, wiping the sweat off of their glistening black bodies.

'You the little nigga, who everybody be talking about got mad luck?' said one of the sweaty hoopers.

‘I don’t know man, I didn’t know I was doing anything special enough to be recognized like that.’

‘Nigga, I’m talking about shootin’ dice. You should come play wit’ us sometime. I’ll show you how a real boss handles his money.’

‘Aight man, maybe. I don’t really play like that anymore though.’

They laughed at him, ‘Whatchu mean? What are you twelve, thirteen? You just gettin’ started. My nigga Red told me you got heart too, you could probably role wit’ us if you got what it take lil’ man.’

Devontae was ready to leave, he hadn’t intended on being initiated into a gang that day and was not sure how to turn down the offer without being disrespectful.

‘Aight man, I’ll think about it.’

‘That’s what’s up. Lil’ nigga gotta think about it. We need smart niggas rollin’ wit’ us. If you ain’t smart, you might as well be dead. I’ll lay a dumb nigga out in two seconds.’

A scuffle broke out on the other end of the court and everyone dropped their towels and ran over to see who the altercation involved. Devontae used the opportunity to leave the courtyard and continue on to the library. The last thing he wanted was to be a part of gang life. Many of his friends were beginning to be curious about the operations; the fast, easy money; the respect; the girls. It was easy for most of them; they had very little structure in their lives. Half of them had inattentive mothers like his and no father around; some were the middle child and got over looked; and some just did not care what their mother, grandmother or aunt had to say; they were going to live their lives in the streets regardless of the cautions that their guardians heeded. It was unfortunate that children were being forced to make life-altering decisions at such a young age but gangs made them feel like they had a functioning family, like somebody truly cared. Either you get killed, kill someone else, or both. They forgot that living was also an option. The thousands of stories in the library reassured Devontae that there were more options than the three his friends felt compelled to choose from.

Black Boy was his book of the week. He could relate to Richard Wright, to his internal struggles; the battles that were necessary to fight in order to be triumphant in the end. It made him dream of being a writer, a man with powerful words and a pen to record them, to document his pervasive thoughts. Thoughts that could potentially touch a kid like him.

The sun was setting as he walked home, carrying "Black Boy" and a few other quick reads. Right before he reached his complex, a red El Dorado pulled up behind him and five men emerged from the vehicle.

'Aye, lil' nigga,' called Red, 'I heard you dissed my boys today. If you ain't trynna be a member of our crew, you ain't shit.'

Devontae turned around, already irritated by Red's rough voice. 'Dawg, I ain't dis yo' niggas, I said I would think about it.'

'Well, what the fuck do you think?'

‘I didn’t have a chance to think about it yet damn nigga, fuck wrong wit’ you? Rollin’ up on me with these silly ass questions? You supposed to be a grown man, out here lookin’ weak as hell.’

‘This lil’ nigga is crazy. What did I tell you about disrespecting me?’ he motioned to his protégés and they walked forward, quickly assembling themselves around Devontae. Devontae dropped his books on the ground and swung the first punch. Everything else after that was blackness. At first, he could feel the blows to the head and to his stomach, like lightning bolts in a merciless storm. When his body hit the ground, the earth shook – or so it seemed – something had changed besides the transformation from intact bones to broken ones. Innocence was drifting away. The kicks to the ribs and legs became like ripples over his body as he lay unconscious. Involuntary convulsions and movements in his fingers resembled those of a fallen boxer, suffering from brain injuries. His entire face was covered in blood, dripping from his mouth and across the pages of Black Boy, staining the words, so that they became illegible. Deep cuts pulsed with red and white as white blood cells and thrombocytes attempted to repair the wounds and protect against foreign pathogens. But even his body’s natural defenses were not fast enough to prevent the rapid blood loss that his library book so conveniently collected and absorbed.

The news spread quickly and soon Cambria came running down the street and outside of the complex, where she found a crowd of spectators surrounding her little brother. She pushed them out of the way and made her way to the ground, taking his upper body in her arms and rocking him back and forth. Her tears stung like acid rain on soiled cheeks. 'Somebody call for an ambulance!' she screamed. 'What are you standing around for? Do something! Help us!'

Some people shuffled away, ashamed of their inaction, others continued to look on and whisper about the terrible condition he was in. They wondered aloud if he would survive or not. Cambria talked to him softly until the ambulance arrived, 'Come on Devontae, look at me, hang in there, everything is gonna be alright.'

At the hospital, Cambria waited in the emergency area shaking her head in disbelief, she had left the twins with a neighbor. 'How could a child who just keeps to himself keep getting attacked by people?' She wasn't surprised when her mother came running into the hospital belligerently calling for her only son. She ran up to the front counter asking anyone and everyone for information, three nurses had to contain her, while they waited for Devontae's doctor to come out. Meanwhile, Cambria just sat observing; the doctors had already informed her that her brother was fine but that he suffered three broken ribs and a broken nose. They said he was lucky to only have those few major injuries, everything else was just bruising and some open wounds. She could see them across the lobby telling her mother the same thing, then they pointed to Cambria and told her she would have to wait an hour or so until she could go see him. But Cambria didn't want to talk to her mother; her disappointment in her mother's late appearance was evident in her facial expression.

‘I’m sorry I’m late, baby!’ said Momma Kiesha as she walked up to give Cambria a hug.

‘It’s whatever, better than last year when it took you three days to figure out that Devontae was in the hospital after he got shot,’ Cambria said, dryly.

‘Sweety, I was actually not where you think I was. I was with Ms. Heath. She should be coming in soon with Nawiri. I have a surprise for you,’ she said happily. Cambria’s faced remained blank.

The emergency room was a sad place, most of the family members looked like they were on the verge of a heart attack, sitting on the edge of their seats, biting their finger nails, waiting for either great or devastating news. There was a man and his son waiting patiently to her right; she noticed that he was merely flipping the pages of the magazine in his hands, neither reading the words nor seeing the pictures; his gaze burned through the paper and into the blue carpet. A woman in a beautiful floral dress had rung the front of the dress so many times that there was a large, imprinted circular wrinkle. The only people who seemed to be holding onto sanity were the very old, many of whom had fallen asleep; and the very young, who went about playing and comforting the adults as if life was going to go on with or without their sick or injured family members. Ms. Heath and Nawiri stepped inside just as the doctors called Cambria and Kiesha into Devontae’s room.

Inside the room, Kiesha gave him a gigantic hug forgetting that three of his ribs were broken. He screamed and she jumped back quickly.

Cambria just held his hand. He tried to move his mouth to say something but his cheeks and lips were swollen. 'I think he's trying to say something,' said Momma Kiesha. 'What's that baby? You want to write it down?' But it was useless; his hands had many cuts and were buried underneath several layers of white gauze. Kiesha told him that Nawiri and her mother were there to see him but he began to move his arms underneath the blankets and shake his head from side-to-side, even his heart rate began to increase on the monitor. It was evident that he did not want Nawiri to see him in such a horrible state. Momma Kiesha walked outside of the room and shook her head 'no' to inform them and went back to sit by his bed. When Cambria stepped outside to use the restroom, Nawiri ran up to her and asked, 'How is he? Is he ok?'

'What do you care?'

'He's my friend. I just want to make sure he's ok before we leave.'

'Why don't you do something useful like pay his medical bill 'cause we don't have no damn health insurance. If you ain't talking about being useful, then you need to go home.'

Nawiri was shocked by Cambria's blunt and rude remarks. She heaved a sigh of disappointment and went back to stand beside her grandmother. 'What did she say?' asked Ms. Heath. 'Nothing,' responded Nawiri, 'let's go home.' They left with heavy hearts and hoped to hear good news about his condition in a few days.

THE PEOPLE

'Love is as love does, and it is our responsibility to give children love. When we love children we acknowledge by our every action that they are not our property, that they have rights – that we respect and uphold their rights. Without justice there can be no love.' – bell hooks *All About Love: New Visions*

Kiesha stayed home for the entire three weeks that Devontae was in the hospital, she was organizing a welcome home party for him and wanted everything to be perfect. When she wasn't knocking on doors, inviting the neighbors or cooking huge dishes of macaroni and cheese, green beans and fried chicken, she was visiting him in the hospital. His swelling had almost completely gone down and he was eating and talking again. On the day of the surprise party, Momma Kiesha and Ms. Heath picked him up from the hospital because Kiesha didn't have a vehicle. He kept asking about Nawiri but they would ignore his questions with more questions for him like, 'How are you feeling?' 'Are you hungry? Do you want to stop for something to eat?' and 'There's a gas station, you want some gum or something?' Devontae was irritated by them ignoring his questions, so he kept quiet for the rest of the ride.

When they opened the front door to his house, there was a thunderous roar, 'SURPRISE!!!!!!!!!!!!!' He almost fell backwards off of the door step, smiling from ear-to-ear, he walked slowly around the room lightly embracing neighbors and giving dap to his boys. Everyone was there, Snappy, Junior, Young John, Ike, Keith, Thomas, Malcolm, Nicholas, Tanya, lil' Zeek, cousin Sherie, Tasha with her newborn baby, Ms. Colts and Mr. Edison from school, Sasha, Ms. Karena, Ms. Robyn, Cambria, the twins, even Mr. Jones other people from their old neighborhood. And finally, there was Nawiri.

She had just traded in her bifocals for a new pair of contacts. Her hair was brushed back into a neat ponytail, from which her natural curls created a beautiful spectacle in the back of her head. She had even applied some lip gloss, which she rarely ever did, making the shine of her smooth skin stand out even more. She waited patiently as he made his way around the room, greeting all of the visitors who had come from near and far to wish him a quick recovery and to chow down of some of his mother's home-cooked soul food. When he finally approached her, they embraced one another unashamedly; it was the longest three weeks of his life, three weeks without seeing her was like a week in prison. He let go of her slowly, feeling a jolting pain in his rib cage. They went on to talk about Tanisha's progress, both very pleased with the results from the new diet. Nawiri seemed to harbor an excitement that Devontae could not quite put his finger on but he would find out soon enough.

The party was remarkable; many more people dropped in once they heard the music and the base bumping, vibrating the complex walls.

Devontae was pleased to see that there were so many people who cared about his health and well-being. He moved slowly through the crowd, greeting his neighbors, friends and family members. On an average day it seemed that no one really cared, perhaps it was all a stunt but he felt good about it regardless. Just as the height of the party began to die down, none other than Red walked through the door, followed by Cambria, who was mysteriously wearing a pair of sunglasses on this warm, summer night. Devontae gave him a grimacing stare as Red walked toward him to express his condolences, 'Aye man, sorry to hear about what happened to you. It's a shame; you gotta watch your back at all times out here in the streets.' Devontae listened to his bullshit and then responded, 'Yeah dawg, especially when the niggas ridin' you are sittin' up in your house drinkin' your cool-aid and fuckin' your sister.' The room was so noisy that no one heard the remarks exchanged; Red smirked and walked away with Cambria following close behind. Devontae shook his head and turned back to Nawiri, who was like a breath of fresh air in the midst of chaos.

'Is that the guy who beat you up?' asked Nawiri.

'Something like that,' Devontae said in a low tone.

'Why don't you go to the police?'

'That's how you get killed for real. I walked away with my life and I plan on holding onto it for a little while longer.'

Nawiri didn't understand, so she just raised her eyebrows, smiled and nodded her head.

Red was a man with a vision. And that vision, simply put, was to control the drug trade in Detroit. In his mind, he reigned over the hood that happened to sit on a large plot of land, none of which he owned – not even one square foot. But it didn't matter to him, as long as he felt like he was running things. His passion for control stemmed from his childhood, a time when he never felt like he controlled anything, not even his own life. A woman found him on her doorstep when he was a week old and subsequently gave him to the foster care system. Spending his entire childhood being moved from home to home, made him feel unstable and more comfortable in the streets, a place that was relatively constant and where he could control his own movements. At the tender age of sixteen, the streets became his permanent home. He answered to only one person, lived by his own rules and anyone who questioned his authority, his movements or his actions was punished, accordingly. No one knew his full story but Red's ruthless nature was apparent in his empty eyes. Devontae's choice was simple – remain silent or prepare to perish.

Streams of people were beginning to leave and the clean-up crew – Kiesha, Ms. Heath, Ms. Karena, Ms. Robyn, Sasha, and Nawiri got to work as Devontae thanked everyone for coming out and walked them to the door. Sasha and Ms. Karena were the next to leave. Ms. Karena was telling Sasha that she had eaten too much and was going to become fat like Oprah and then struggle to lose the weight for the rest of her life. Sasha was tuning her out, thinking about all the numbers she had pulled that night. Everywhere she went, the attention she received from boys her own age and men much older was becoming overwhelming for her.

As Nawiri, Ms. Robyn and Ms. Heath were approaching the front door, to leave, they stopped and Ms. Heath asked Kiesha, 'Are you ready now?'

Momma Kiesha's face was serious as she thought deeply. Finally, she looked up and said, 'I think I am.' Then, she turned to her children and told them to sit down on the couch.

Devontae and Cambria were very nervous. Ms. Heath and Momma Kiesha pulled up chairs to sit in front of the kids and Ms. Robyn directed Nawiri to go sit in the car. 'But Ma!' protested Nawiri. 'No buts, just go!' Nawiri walked slowly to the car, with her head down feeling left out and isolated.

Momma Kiesha cleared her throat as she prepared to embark on a long explanation to her children; she readjusted her skirt took, crossed her legs, then uncrossed them. Ran her fingers through her hair a few times, took a deep breath and then she began, 'Over the last five years, I have not been there for you guys. Cambria, how lucky am I to have such a mature and responsible daughter, who has held our family together? You have been forced to play a role that no child should ever have to play. Devontae, you have stayed focused in school even without a parent there to support you, guide you, or put pressure on you. It's amazing. And that shows that you have way more drive than the average kid and you are gonna be something special. I just know it! Anisha, baby girl, you remind me so much of myself, never complain, just role with the punches, goin' wit' the flow. And Tanisha…' Kiesha began to cry, 'I have been most unfair to you. It's a wonder you are still alive, the way you have not received the type of care and attention that you need. I have been so blessed with four children who have survived and weathered a storm that not many children can do and still come out with their sanity. But I've realized with the help of this beautiful woman, Ms. Heath, that I can control what I do. That I don't have to let the past dictate my present or my future and that everyone has a breaking point. I reached mine five years ago but I don't ever want my children to reach that point, so I know what I have to do. I gotta get myself together. I gotta get straight, so that I can be the loving, supportive and attentive mother that I want to be and that I know I can be.' She surveyed their faces to get a feel for their attitudes. Interested maybe. Receptive not quite yet. Their eyes were wide with surprise and disbelief. To reassure them that every word spoken was true and genuine, she went on to talk about how love can overcome all obstacles and how her love for them was the driving force for her recovery. The reason why she knew there was no turning back from here. The following silence was so still that you could hear her tear drops falling with a soft thud on her denim jeans.

Kiesha went on to tell them her life story. She didn't want to make excuses for herself but she needed them to understand how and why she could allow a drug addiction to take control of her life. Working with Ms. Heath for two months to get to the point where she could understand it herself was a grueling challenge and it would take even longer for her to build the courage to express it fully to others.

'Starting next week, I'm moving to a rehabilitation center about two hours outside of the city and I will need to live there for at least a year. When I come back, they're gonna help me find a job and get a new place in Brightmoor, where we can all live. But in the meantime, Ms. Heath and Ms. Robyn have graciously offered up their home to you, my beautiful children, for the time that I'm away. So, what do you think?'

The kids were not sure how to respond. Never in his wildest dreams did Devontae think he would be able to live in a house like Nawiri's before he was twenty one and especially not in the same house with her! Anisha seemed to be excited for a change, even though she didn't know what all of this meant exactly. But Cambria looked utterly disgusted. She had been taking care of herself and her siblings for five years and even though she hated that her childhood was being torn away from her, this was the way of life that she had gotten accustomed too. No rules, no curfews, no questions, no drama, no punishments, no expectations, no homework checks, no clothing checks, no inquiries, just pure freedom. It was the type of life every kid wished for but no kid was ready for. And even though she'd spent five years wishing for her mother to get clean and come back home for good, now she wasn't so sure.

'Cambria, sweetheart, are you ok?'

'No, I gotta go,' she jumped up before anyone could hold her back and ran out of the house.

SEX 4 SUGA

Sasha was sick of her mother. The air in their house was suffocating her with cigarette smoke, unrealistic demands and foul accusations. Sasha missed the summer days when her mother sat on the porch and talked with Ms. Kiesha and Ms. Heath and Ms. Robyn. On those days, she had been much more calm and pleasant. She would even sing in the car and ask Sasha to join in or stop by the mall to pick up matching t-shirts. But those days had come to an end. Once Devontae was hospitalized, Ms. Karena decided she didn't want Sasha hanging around in that area, in fact she didn't even want Sasha to be Devontae's friend anymore but Sasha was of course not going to sever their relationship just because he got beat up. Besides, she was set on being the bridesmaid in he and Nawiri's wedding.

The insults were becoming far more intense than Sasha ever thought she could bear; she found herself sneaking out the house more and more often these days.

'I thought I told you to vacuum, why do I still see dirt in this corner! You may be ok with living like a filthy animal but I don't live like that! Get the vacuum and do the whole damn floor over!' Ms. Karena screamed.

'Yes Ma'am.'

'What was that?'

'I said yes ma'am,' repeated Sasha.

'Don't yes Ma'am me, who the fuck do you think you're talking to? I heard that attitude in your voice! You think you can disrespect me in my own house? You have no idea what I'm capable of! And you know what, I know you been having sex you little whore. I seen all them numbers you brought home from Devontae's party. I threw all of'em away. You think I'm gonna let some niggas run a train on my daughter? Didn't I teach you to respect yourself? You low down floosy. Ain't no hoes gon' be livin' in my house, I'll kick your ass right out on the street. I don't give a fuck where you go!'

Sasha shed tears on the carpet as she re-vacuumed the entire first floor. It was a never-ending cycle of verbal abuse. She flinched whenever her mother walked into the same room, anticipating the verbal blows to her self-confidence. What left her the most dumb-founded was that her mother was so nice to her younger sister. She wondered if perhaps Niamako hadn't reached an age her mother felt was appropriate to treat her like a slave or if she would always have the privilege of being the princess of the household. Anything that Niamako spilled or destroyed was always blamed on Sasha. She took the fall for her mother's mistakes, her sister's mistakes and even her father's mistakes.

'You think you gon' control me like your father tried to control me? You better think again or your face will catch the back of this hand if you even so much as look at me like you got something to say! As long as I'm payin' the bills, then you keep your mouth shut! You hear me? Shut!'

'Yes Ma'am.'

'I thought I said don't say shit to me!'

Ms. Karena worked herself into such a rage every day that she chain smoked like a factory chimney. Her voice cracked as she yelled through the thick smoke bellowing out of her mouth. Her evening scotch usually enlivened the insults and death threats for an hour or so until she became very hungry and then very, very sleepy. This allowed for easy escapes, as Sasha just walked right out of the front door to visit one of her summer lovers.

Brandon was her favorite. He was tall, funny, dark chocolate with defined muscles to match. He was the wide receiver for Malcolm X High School and third fastest sprinter in the state. Even though he was an all-star, he treated her with the most respect out of any of the other guys she dealt with. He would sometimes even listen to her problems and give her back massages to ease the tension. Sometimes, they would watch the sunset when Ms. Karena went to sleep early or walk to Dairy Queen to get smoothies. Many jealous girls watched them with envy in their eyes as she fed him spoon fulls of frozen strawberry ice. She learned a lot about diligence from him and believing in herself. Before him, she had just followed Nawiri and did well in school because it just seemed like the right thing to do, not because she believed in herself. So consumed with Brandon, she stopped paying as much attention to the other guys. Brandon was slightly weary of dating a fourteen year old, considering he was sixteen going on seventeen, but her beauty propelled him onward.

With him, she didn't have to sneak into the abandoned Mustang in the driveway, he let her come up to his room. She browsed his CD selection; he listened to all the good stuff. Mos Def, Common, Jay-Z, Outkast, Shyne, Tupac, Biggie, Master P, K-OS, Wu-Tang Clan, Nas, Snoop Dogg, Lauryn Hill. He even had old school hip hop like LL Cool J, Afrikaa Bambataa, and Grand Master Flash. Posters of famous athletes like Micheal Jordon, Micheal Vick and The Fab 5 cluttered the walls and a beautifully polished football sat on the window seal signed by Detroit's own Barry Sanders.

'Why does this look so new?' asked Sasha.

'My Dad gave it to me before he passed away,' said Brandon nostalgically. 'You can pick it up if you want, just don't scratch it, or else I'll have to tickle you to death,' he teased.

'Nah, that's ok, I don't wanna risk it. I can't handle too much tickling,' she smiled.

‘Aww man but I wanted to tickle you. Can I still do it even if you don’t pick up the ball?’

‘Hmmm, well. It depends on what you’ll let me do to you.’

Brandon was smiling from ear to ear as she walked toward him. ‘You are not fourteen,’ he said aloud. His teenage hormones raging with desire for this young beauty. The light from the sun shining through the window illuminated her features; she was perfect to him. She sat on his lap and gave him a long, passionate kiss. Then she continued, ‘Now, you can do whatever you want.’

Didn't Cha Know

Move-out was a daunting task, especially for the twins who had relied on their sister for everything. They constantly asked where Cambria was and when she would return, crying as they left their home, the only place Cambria would know where to find them. Kiesha thought of leaving a note with the new address, just in case, but decided that was not a safe idea, considering anyone could open the screen door and find it. The police were still searching but had been unsuccessful in every aspect besides knowing who she was with - Red. Knowing she was with Red made the neighbors more uncooperative; some even claimed that they had never even seen Cambria before in their lives even though she had been playmates with their children for years. Even the police were aware of Red's 'high-profile' status within the area and were not expecting to find much useful information in the projects. Red was what the police referred to as a floater, he had many places of residence, so it was extremely difficult to track him down. Cambria could have been at one of these places or none of them, there was no way to know, especially without any informants.

The school administrators did not have any information on Cambria's whereabouts either. It was as if she had disappeared into thin air without any clear traces and the police were not concerned enough to follow more dead ends than necessary. Her face became a poster in the police station, so that she would not be forgotten but the active search was coming to an end. They told the family that they would keep them updated and moved on to the next case.

Most of the furniture was put into storage, to be taken out upon Kiesha's return. They carried large boxes full of kitchenware and toys out of the house. The living room couch, television set, china cabinet, beds, dressers, tables and chairs, pictures, empty frames and clothing were all being transported to storage. When they were finished, Devontae, Kiesha, Anisha and Tanisha stood in the living room gazing at its emptiness. This place had been their safe haven, their livelihood; they didn't see the dust covering the carpet or the scratches on the walls, instead they only saw memories. Kiesha was envisioning the time when her ex-boyfriend, Clifford, the twins' father, had come home with the most jubilant smile. He had landed a job in one of the car factories and took everyone to get ice cream to celebrate his good fortune; when they got back home, Anisha spilled her strawberry ice cream on the tan carpet. The stain was still there, Kiesha stared at it and saw the tilted ice cream still lingering on the floor before they cleaned the area. Then, she turned her attention to a particular hole in the wall that remained from one of her favorite family pictures. Tanisha kept repeating the word Bobo, which was the lazy hound that used to lie on their front porch when he was hiding from his owner. Devontae was thinking of the summers when he was six and seven; they would roast marshmellows over the grill outside and then come into the living room where they assembled s'mores and Momma

Kiesha would tell them spooky stories about werewolves and dinosaur-size tarantulas. Then, they would run back outside to make more marshmellows and back into the living room to hear more stories. After about three trips, they would fall asleep on the living room floor and Kiesha would carry them up to their bedrooms.

Devontae set up his belongings in the apartment above Ms. Robyn's garage. She was sad to give up the space that had made for such a perfect office and relaxation zone but was willing to let Devontae reside there for the time being. She had considered giving him one of the bedrooms in the house but had observed the same affection between he and Nawiri that Sasha had picked up on in the very beginning. So, she decided against it.

'What's the deal with you and Devontae?' Ms. Robyn asked Nawiri, inquisitively.

'We're just friends,' said Nawiri with a nonchalant shrug.

'So, you don't like him like him?'

'Mom! Stop acting like a teenager! Snooping all in my business,' Nawiri teased.

They laughed. 'Well, just to be on the safe side, I'm give him my office above the garage.'

'What?!?! Aww, man. That's no fair, he gets that whole place to himself? Why can't I live out there?'

'Nawiri, please. Your room is big enough. Plus, he's a boy, I think he can hold his own out there. Don't worry you'll have your own apartment soon enough, in about five years. Boy, I can't wait for that day! Woohoo!' she laughed.

'You know you can't live without me,' Nawiri hugged her mom around the neck as she sat at the kitchen counter, kissing her on the forehead.

'Oh, but I could.'

'Nope, you couldn't, definitely not.'

They went back and forth jokingly but the decision had been made. Devontae loved his new space. He had his own bedroom, kitchenette, living room and bathroom. He hung up his uniform, three pairs of jeans, and his jacket in the closet. Then, he folded his random assortment of Sean Jean, FUBU and Guess t-shirts and placed them in the dresser. He didn't have much to furnish his living quarters but he used his own bed in the bedroom, the living room area was already furnished and the kitchen was stocked with a few pots and pans, cereal was in the cupboard and some strange-looking health food snacks in the refrigerator. Seeing there was no television, radio or other form of entertainment, Devontae went to the house and asked Ms. Heath for a book to read.

'Why, of course! What you want child? Fiction? Non-fiction? Mystery? History? A love story, perhaps?'

She led him to their library, which he had not seen during his first visit to their house. It was a massive home library, filled with Encyclopedias, novels, how-to books, religious texts from around the world, books about African American history, theater, dance, politics, and a whole section dedicated to health books from recipes to pilates stretches. Devontae was in heaven.

'Can I come here anytime and get a book?' he asked, still in disbelief.

'Of course! Well, not in the middle of the night but anytime during the day, this whole room is open to you for endless exploration. I haven't even read half of these books. My daughter, Ms. Robyn, just collects them, knowing that one day we'll get to all of them. I pick up one to read about every two weeks. Slowly but surely, I'm getting there.'

She left him alone to look around; he had the entire Saturday to read. Nawiri was at swimming practice and then she had piano lessons later in the day. Ms. Heath had decided to start preparing GFCF meals for Tanisha, after she found out that the kids had stolen her meal plan for Autistic children. She commended them for their efforts but felt that such a project should be left up to dieticians and parents. She told them to just focus on school and that she would take over from where they had left off. Anisha had gone to play at a new friend's house across the street.

He walked along the walls reading book titles; they all seemed so interesting. The Qu'ran, the Bible, Tao te Ching, Shakespeare, all of Toni Morrison's books, Things Fall Apart, Little House on the Prairie, The Great Gatsby, Invisible Man, Native Son, A Fairwell to Arms, the

Grapes of Wrath, Megatrends, The Famished Road, Waiting to Exhale and many more. He settled with two to start with The Positive Philosophy by Auguste Comte, and the Communist Manifesto by Karl Marx. He went back to his room, sat on the couch, opened an orange soda, the last one he would probably drink in this household, and opened the first book.

Time seemed to collapse as he read for hours without respite, engulfed in the pages filled with knowledge and information. He could feel himself being lifted above worldly aggression and stress, his situation had not changed but his reality seemed different to him now. Struggle was still a burden but now he saw it as a necessary experience for restoration. In the morning, Ms. Heath sent Nawiri to check on him because he had missed dinner. She knocked and there was no answer, so she knocked harder. Eventually, there was a scrambling at the door as Devontae struggled with the locks.

'Where have you been? You out here starving yourself?'

'Naw, what time is it? It's clearly not too early for you to be out here harassing me,' he teased as he opened the door to let her in.

'My grandma sent me out here to see if you were still alive because you missed dinner last night.'

'O yeah, I was so into this book called, 'The Positive Philosophy.' I got it out of your Mom's library. I can't believe you have so many books in your own house. Have you read any of them?'

'Of course! But I like fiction the best. Have you read Native Son? I think you would like it, it's by Richard Wright.'

'Oh, for real? Yeah, I like Richard Wright! I finished Black Boy when I got out of the hospital. I can relate to him on a lot of levels,' Devontae was standing in the kitchen doorway awkwardly. 'I'm sorry, uhm, do you want something to drink? There's some apple juice in here, and I think there's some grape juice left too.' He opened the refrigerator and pulled out both bottles of juice, waiting for Nawiri's reply.

She laughed, 'It's ok. We live in the same house; you don't have to treat me like a guest. Besides there's way more juice and food in the house. Why don't you come inside in thirty minutes, so we can eat breakfast together?'

'Ok, cool, sounds good. I'm starving since I didn't really eat dinner last night. I had some of this dip your mom left in the refrigerator out here. I was a little skeptical at first because of the green mold color but after I started, I couldn't stop! It was so good.'

Nawiri smiled, 'Welcome to the good life! Once you go healthy, you can never go back. That was spinach and avocado dip by the way, not mold, silly.'

She walked down the outdoor stairs of the garage and back into the house. Devontae watched her as she left. She turned around and caught him staring, 'I'll make you some more guacamole for lunch,' she yelled and retreated into the house.

It was a strange feeling, living with Nawiri, Ms. Robyn and Ms. Heath. The air was fresher, the moon and stars shone a little brighter at night, even water took on a new magical quality. He had originally thought that the house, or a house like this one, would solve everything. That it would erase the pains impressed upon him by poverty, that it would give him something to take pride in and that it would even give his life more meaning. Though his awe had not yet worn thin, he now realized that the house was not doing these things for him but it was the smiles, the warm laughter, and the genuine concern for his well-being, covering him in a blanket of love that made all the little things in life feel ten times sweeter.

THE COOLEST

The second week of school was still exciting and new. The kids were excited to see one another after a three month break. They had new jokes, new uniforms, new hairstyles, and new shoes. Many of the students had grown two or three inches, the girls were developing and the boys were paying attention to every new feature. Even Nawiri came back with a new look, Devontae was surprised when she emerged from the house with large hoop earrings, curly hair running down her back, a new pleated skirt that she had purchased with the money she had saved for new uniform clothes, a new pair of Rockports and a fly pair of sunglasses she got for ten dollars at the African Art Festival they went to on Labor Day weekend. Devontae picked his jaw up off the ground just in time to open the car door for her.

'Wow, I don't even know what to say,' said Devontae trying not to let his eyes wander.

Nawiri laughed, 'I'll take that as a compliment. I decided that this would be the last year that people make fun of me for being a dork. I'm a young woman now and I'm going to wear clothes that fit!' she said defiantly and slipped into the car. Devontae laughed and climbed into the back seat. He had also purchased a few new school items with the money he had left over from gambling. The rest of it was still tucked away in the bank. He tried hard not to ask for anything from Ms. Heath or Ms. Robyn and insisted that if they gave him any money that he provide some service in return. So, his household chores became fixing appliances, mowing the lawn, watering the garden, power washing the wooden deck and other miscellaneous tasks. In the Fall, he would be in charge of raking leaves and cleaning the gutters and in the winter his main chore would be shoveling the snow.

The classrooms were so hot that the children grew irritable and restless by the end of the day. They threw pencils at one another, drew on desks and on each other. The girls had hearts and stars on their hands with short sentences like, 'I love Derek,' or 'Superstar Dime Diva.' Nawiri and Sasha split a granola bar and put rhinestones on their faces, watching Steven Jones teach Devontae how to make more complicated beats on the table. It was a painstaking skill, one that only endurance could explain the ability of a person to continue on, when their knuckles were feeling raw and turning red. The boys would make beats on the table and freestyle over them during homeroom, before and after school. Then, they continued outside of the school while they waited for their parents to pick them up. Devontae had never wanted to freestyle with the boys at school. Before, he had his neighborhood friends but those days were over. He could visit them but it wasn't the same. He couldn't just walk around the corner and knock on Young John or Junior's doors, so he had to find a new crew to practice with. For most of the kids, rap was a leisurely activity but for Devontae, it was a necessary part of his well-being.

One day during lunch, Devontae decided not to play football because there was a battle scheduled to take place in Mr. Edison's classroom. The students had hyped up the event so much that even the teachers were interested in seeing the spectacle. The students rushed to eat their lunches in the cafeteria and ran up to the classroom only to see that some students had eaten their lunches in the classroom and there was very little space left for the newcomers. The crowd flooded out into the hallway. Teachers, who were concerned about potential chaos, instructed the kids to move the 'event' to the playground, where they would have room for everyone. The crowd followed the contestants, one of whom was Devontae, outside and formed a circle around them. Devontae looked around for Nawiri and found her standing reasonably close to the front. He wanted to make sure she was close enough to hear him. Otherwise, he would have pulled her closer to the center of the circle.

There were three sets of battles lined up: Steven vs. Derek, Andrew vs. Devontae, and two girls Tierra vs. Erika. The crowd thickened, everyone was anxious for the show of the 'Century.' Even the teachers between commands for students to behave, were listening for the start of the beat and the ensuing lyrical flow. Steven and Derek stepped to the middle and Devontae started to beat on a desk they had managed to bring outside. The crowd went silent as the beat became louder and overpowered their voices, it was like an African drum, the rhythm was consistent and intoxicating. The girls resisted the urge to dance as they listened in for the start of the first verse. They decided heads would go first and flipped a coin. It was Derek, he listened intently to the beat and proceeded confidently:

I got swag like I'm Kool Herc, living on a poster

Gucci bag for my girl and some thugged out loafers

I'll bang wit' any Nigga that try to step to my flow

I'm a fire breathing dragon, blow you out the back do'

Inevitable disaster like Hurricane Andrew

Nigga anything you can do, I can do…better.

Settin' shit ablaze, like your wack ass sweater.

I know the whole encyclopedia, you still working on letters.

Call me Mr. Schitzo, I'm on some insane shit

Can't get nothin' by me, man I never miss a lick

Ask ya girl Teressa what we did last night

Still got a bump right here cause she was bitin my lip

I see the rage in your eyes but you ain't talking bout shit

This a real nigga battle, don't go out like no bitch

Your boys out here watchin', don't embarrass your clique

I know it's hard to find inspiration when you battlin' me

So, just ask me for some help, if you need some G

The crowd went crazy, cheering for Derek and prompting Steven to come back or go home. Steven was focused, nodding his head and swaying from side-to-side. Andrew took over the beat for Devontae and the battle continued.

I been in the game for a minute but I don't need no applause
The celebration is in my lyrics, flow so smooth with no bars
I got a knack for knowledge, I don't need no fancy cars
Chillin' like a villain on my way to the stars
I think yo' rap was cute with those little catchy phrases
But I still know know yo' mama, on a first name bases
It's true what they say, a nigga can't catch a break
But I'ma hold it down, throw it down and mirk niggas actin fake
I'ma collectible, intellectual with so much flavor
Take a puff, then pass it on, like I'm signin' a waiver
I'm high tech savvy with a low cut fade
Bought a necklace for my girl made with diamonds and jade
I'm only fourteen years but I'm getting' highly paid
Laughin' at broke niggas like Derek and Wade
I'm so on fire that I even sweat in my sleep
For breakfast, lunch and dinner, I pick niggas like you to eat

The audience erupted again into cheers and applause. Then, quieted down for the vote. Tina, the girl chosen to be the coordinator of the competition, placed her hand over Derek's head and the roar was so loud that it appeared to awaken the entire outdoors. Birds went fluttering out of trees and squirrels ran up them. Then, she placed her hand over Steven and they also cheered exuberantly, but the excitement was clearly weaker. So, Derek was proclaimed winner of that round. Next up was Tierra vs. Erika. They stepped into the ring, Derek took over the beat and Erika went in without hesitation. She was thought to be very feminine for a rapper, her voice reminding many of a young Left Eye.

Infidel, galactic us, I'm flier than an octopus

Dudes, they think they runnin' this but then they bend and kiss my…

(Pause, smile, nods head) …foot

I could never be an architect, too scared I'd fall and break my neck

I'd rather be a poor girl spreading knowledge to the world

Nothing like Tierra Diva – Louie bags and temple curls

Down to earth Mami, with a knack for smokin' weed

Got that kush, that blueberry, and some watermelon seed

Flying over Babylon, that's all I really need

Apple pie, swisher sweet, candy cane, lemon drop

Vanilla bean ice cream, maraschino cherry on top

I'll spice ya life up, with my sugary blessings

But I'm pressed for time, gotta teach Tierra some lessons

Just like I clean the house, my flow so damn neat

And if you see me take a break, don't even think about my seat

This brown sugar throne was custom-made for me

Well, I guess you could try but consequences run deep

Tierra smiled; she looked as if she had been waiting her whole life for this moment. Breathing steadily, she looked at her opponent and almost felt sorry for the verbal lashing that was about to occur but not enough to prevent the words from slipping out of her mouth.

Never in my life have I heard a flow so whack

Ask the whole world, it's not opinion, it's a fact

I see you trynna hate but steady jocking my style

Next day, I see you shopping in my favorite store isle

Then you leave quick and start looking for the fake shit,

Fall apart so fast, girl you might as well make it

Yo flow so immature, what's an infant to a child?

You crawlin' on all fours, I been walking for a while

See ain't no disrespect, I'm trynna show you how I do

Maybe we can try tomorrow, so u can practice after school

I'm on some next level shit, travelin' through the atmosphere

I see them bones shaking, yeah I recognize the fear

So strong, I'm like a mountain, you won't see me shedding tears

I'm a beast not a burden, let me make it very clear

First albums gonna drop in about four to five years

Don't worry baby girl, I'll send a copy in the mail

The crowd was in shock, pure shock. Most of the students had underestimated the ability of the female rappers. Believing that they would show an inferior level of creative prowess in a freestyle battle compared to that of the boys. But the audience had been deceived by their preconceived notions. History was in the making as these young artists had showed up and showed out. Positive vibes and jittery excitement was like a gravitational force pulling bodies toward the center of the circle. The girls were glowing with pride and satisfaction with their performances, as were their new admirers and soon to be courtiers. After recovering order from side conversations and animated undertones, they proceeded with the same voting process and found Tierra to be the winner in a very close race.

Lastly, but certainly not least, Devontae and Andrew stepped into the circle center. They were the most acclaimed freestylers in the school, known for their intellectual approach, clever phrasing and unique rhymes. The crowd was dead silent; no one wanted to miss a single beat or syllable. Devontae felt the same heightening of his senses that he had felt during the first night of shooting dice in Young John's basement. The sun shone intensely, sweat beads forming on foreheads and under armpits but the people were all unaware, or were simply indifferent to the funk. This battle would go down in the history of the school, so they made the conscious decision to stay faithful to the moment and ignored their sticky bodies. The beat started and Devontae closed his eyes while Andrew started his verse:

It's an interesting equation when you add it all together

Young mind, switching things up and making it clever

I'm as live as a wire, flip, lighter than a feather, whip

Sour cream and onion, dip, niggas riding all on my – tip

I would never front, man I represent the D

A city hibernating, comes alive in my dreams

People under scrutiny, ignoring cracks and seams

Bringing us together not the money but our Blackness

What you see me raising in the air that's my Black fist

They tell me keep on talkin' and I'll end up on the Black list

Then I say fuck'em, let'em taste some of my black dick

I'm sick of their religious and political antics

Tellin' me who, how, when, where and what to do

And when I ask questions, there are few that they can prove

I won't disrespect my man cause I like his flow too

I ain't trynna get votes with low blows and cheap moves

I'd rather flow so nice, so you can get into the groove

But check it, ya girl is smiling, she's thinking that I'm smooth

Devontae glanced at Nawiri as she quickly turned any remnants of a smile into a serious frown and then to a surprised, bewildered look as he gazed at her through the crowd. He had expected Andrew to say something about her, in reference in their encounter during the previous school year with Nawiri standing between the two of them as the prize possession. Devontae winked at her, she smiled instinctively and winked back, then he looked back to the ground to clear his mind. Creative lines began to fill blank space like that of a scribe's quill on papyrus. Transposed instantaneously into spoken words. In sync movements of his thoughts, tongue and mouth to form the perfect pronunciation and emphasis on words and phrases.

I got four or five dollars when I walk up on the scene
Best believe its gon' triple with the knowledge that I bring
Then I step up to the front, they expecting me to lead
Get addicted to my swag, Andrew say he'll never leave
I'm not afraid to bleed, I'll succeed through sweat and tears
Ain't no quick fixes, work my way up through the years
They love the embellishment of my intelligent word assortment
I leave them hoes alone, so I ain't fuckin' wit' abortion
Everything I do, yeah I do it for a reason
Stay loyal to my niggas, you won't see me up for treason
I'm a living God, give you something to believe in
Ain't no room for games, I stay grinding through the seasons
I'm like a rough lesion, a feign man, a bonified weed man
I sieze 'em, I tease 'em and be remise if I don't please 'em
Way faster than reform, settin' examples for the norm
No sleepin' on the job, you may miss the quiet storm
My flow so magnetic, pulling eye balls out the socket
Pull yo' pants up nigga, I see them lyrics in yo' pocket

Andrew had a horrified look of embarrassment, which quickly turned into a sly smirk as he pulled his pants up and waited for the verdict. The crowd seemed dissatisfied with the performance; they had been waiting for the punch lines of the century but had only been fed subtle blows woven into metaphorical phrases. Devontae and Andrew had agreed to battle on these terms, each preferring to show off their ability to create meaningful verses in freestyle form as opposed to deteriorating the confidence of their opponent. Although each of them had taken the liberty to step slightly outside of that boundary, they remained content with the finished product. The crowd cheered loudest for Devontae, qualifying him for the semifinals with the other two winners, which would take place the next day.

The lunch period had been exhausting for everyone; the rhyming, the beating, the cheering and yelling, and even some dancing, all underneath the heat of the September sun had drained the students and teachers alike. Devontae walked into the school talking with his competitors about possibly recording a mixtape together, when Mr. Edison pulled him aside. 'Hey man, can I talk to you real quick? I heard you out there; your lyrics were fly man. I used to do a little rhyming back in the day myself. I'd like to talk to you about something after school, if you have a few minutes.'

Devontae was confused, he couldn't possibly be getting in trouble for cursing because all of the other students had used those words as well. He agreed reluctantly, just as Nawiri approached. Mr. Edison walked away and made room for her to give him a gigantic bear hug. She was very proud of his performance and surprised at the same time, as she had never seen him rap or better yet, freestyle. 'That was really impressive,' she spoke with starry eyes. 'Thank you, it really means a lot to me that you liked it,' Devontae responded. Sasha echoed Nawiri's congratulations, 'Yeah, it was good. You should have been harsher on Andrew though, I know you can go in harder than that.'

Devontae smiled, 'Yeah, I probably can, maybe I'll do a little more of that next time.'

As they walked to class, he couldn't help but to wonder what he had done this time. The last time he had been called into Mr. Edison's classroom after school was for detention when Nawiri had been completing his homework assignments in the beginning of eighth grade. He had been hoping to start off this school year on a better foot, with no new injuries, no fighting, even gambling was on his list of activities to discontinue. And even though Cambria was still missing, he felt more hope for the future than he ever had before. So, trouble in school was certainly not an item on his to-do-list.

Hot and tired, Devontae walked down the hallway slowly, feeling the weight of his steps as he approached Mr. Edison's classroom after school. He told Nawiri to tell Ms. Heath that she could leave without him and that he would take the bus but when Nawiri delivered the message, Ms. Heath insisted that they wait for him. Devontae saw Sasha marching down the hallway and jogged to catch up with her, 'Where you goin?' he asked nosily.

'It's a secret,' she responded, hurriedly.

'Well, is it a coincidence that we're walking in the same direction? We might be going to the same place.'

'Maybe, maybe not,' said Sasha playfully.

'Look at you, acting all V.I.P. I bet you five dollars, we're going to the same place.'

‘But I don’t have five dollars.’

They arrived at Mr. Edison’s doorway and stopped. ‘So, is this your final destination?’ Devontae asked, smiling like he had won the bet that they hadn’t finalized. ‘Hawww, yes! I’m glad I didn’t bet you.’

They entered the classroom, where ten of their ninth grade counterparts sat quietly in front of three teachers – Mr. Edison, Mr. Johnson and Mrs. Colts. The room had an eerie silence that made the students quite uncomfortable. Two more students entered behind them, one of which was Andrew from the freestyle battle.

‘Good afternoon students, I think we have everyone here now with the exception of one who was absent today. We have asked the fifteen of you to join us today for a very special announcement. We are proud to tell you that you have been chosen out of the three hundred students in your class to compete in the prestigious Powerful Words competition. Through your creative writing, colloquial expression and apparent interest in the arts, we believe that you are the fifteen students who deserve the opportunity to compete for this award. The first place prize is a full scholarship to the most prestigious private high school in the State or a Bond if you choose not to attend. Up to five boys and five girls can receive the award. I need to hear from each of you by the end of the week whether or not you are interested in participating. The deadline is in late December, so you have a while to write your essays. The prompt is quite broad; all they ask is that you relate the essay or poem to your own life in a reflective way and that you talk about what you want to be when you grow up and why you are interested in attending their high school. Are there any questions?'

Andrew raised his hand, 'How many words does it have to be?'

'It can be anywhere from 500 to 1000 words. And please guys, we implore you not to tell all of your friends, we like to surprise the students and teachers every year with the names of the contestants and the names of the winners.'

'How much money is the cash prize?' asked Devontae.

'It's about $40,000 dollars but if you choose to attend the school, then the scholarship will cover their $60,000 4-year tuition. And let me be clear, they are not just going to hand you kids $40,000 cash; they are going to give it to you in the form of a bond that you can use toward your college education.'

The students were surprised, nervous and excited about the challenge. For many of them, it was their first time being acknowledged for their talent and they were eager to prove themselves worthy of such an honor. Sasha, on the other hand, was weary of the selection, 'Why me? Why not Nawiri?' she thought. For someone who had been so secretive about her life, she was reluctant to share her personal reflections on her life and questioned why any other person would be interested in it. 'How many people in total are allowed to enter the competition?' asked Sasha.

'Well, there are three other middle schools in the city for whom the scholarship is open and fifteen students at each school can apply. So, that would make sixty students total, ten of whom will be winners. That means you have a one in six chance to win, those are wonderful odds,' replied Mrs. Colts.

The kids were dismissed; they walked slowly outside, thinking of intro sentences and of topics that were most important to them. Devontae and Sasha decided it was best to tell Nawiri now, so that she could use the entire school year to get over the fact that she had not been chosen. But Devontae got into the back seat of the Mercedes and couldn't bring himself to tell the truth. He told them Mr. Edison wanted some help cleaning up his classroom, deciding to tell Nawiri the real story later.

BUTTERFLY

It was half past ten. The wall clock ticked annoyingly as Sasha tossed and turned in her sleep. She could hear the sirens outside on the main streets, some people were still outside, laughing and joking on their porches and the watchful trees were rustling across the street. Tired of fighting sleep, she lie on her back, eyes wide open, staring at the ceiling. There was a light that caught her attention, it was coming from one of the glow in the dark stars that she had stuck on the ceiling many years ago. She watched it as it seemed to turn its glow on and off. Flipping through her countless journals had put her to sleep early. It was her first attempt at reflection in a long time, trying to gather her random thoughts into a cohesive, all-inclusive five hundred word summary about life, her life specifically. Not knowing where to begin, what would be appropriate to share, or where to end was the dilemma that kept her awake and fixated on the lone flashing ceiling star.

Ms. Karena had just recently bought Sasha her first cell phone. It was a black flip phone with a blue background; it even had walkie-talkie capabilities. She reached for it, to look at the time, and noticed a missed call; it was from Brandon. He'd left a voicemail asking if she wanted to come over but it had been over three hours and the last few visits had been increasingly painful, so she shut the phone and placed it back on the night stand.

The minutes seemed to pass slowly, as her mind wandered through space. She tried to keep her thoughts focused on the contest but they continued to stubbornly drift to faraway places. One of which was a beautiful forest; a winding path created itself just for her, where the tallest trees offered protection from the sun and she stopped to pick berries, oranges, mangos and bananas from the trees as she made her way through the thick forest on a seemingly endless path. She laughed for no reason when blue jays chirped and hid behind trees, watching her closely and jumped when small, emerald green lizards crossed her path. She even went as far as to chase after them. Upon coming to a clearing, the tall grass seemed to stretch for miles, so she ran as fast as she could, closing her eyes and letting the wind roar in her ears. Her senses were alive with the smell of lilac flowers, her arms drifted out to the sides and caught the blades of grass. The soft ground molded itself to the soles of her feet. She opened her eyes when she realized she was no longer running but flying, only to see that she was actually falling into a black abyss. Some of the rocks on the sides held television screens and various electronic devices – stoves, lamps, computers, cars, and even a factory chimney. Becoming increasingly hot, she looked down and saw molten lava. Sweating and heaving, she pried her eyes open just before contact.

Sasha lay in the bed, panting, thanking God for her escape from death. She picked up her phone, it was now half past eleven. She dialed Brandon and he answered sleepily, 'Hello?'

'Hey baby, you sleep?'

'Yeah, kind of.'

'Oh ok, I just had a bad dream. Can you talk for a few minutes?'

She could hear some rustling in the background and then a light voice asked, 'Who is that?'

'Who the fuck is that?!' Sasha sat up in the bed; her heart was racing with jealousy and suspicion.

'Nobody, I'll call you tomorrow.'

'No, Brandon, wait!' But it was too late, he had already hung up the phone. She sat in a state of hysteria, from a near death experience in her dream to a heart-breaking one in reality. She had other things she needed to talk to him about besides the dream, like the fact that she missed her menstrual period in August. At first she waited, thinking that it was only late but it was now approaching mid-September and there was nothing, not even a spot. She was scared; she held her knees, rocking back-and-forth and eventually fell asleep with her head tilted on the backboard, in direct line of sight with the blinking star on the ceiling.

In the morning, Ms. Karena took the girls to the Simmons' house and left them there to hang out with the other children, while she and Ms. Robyn went to work out at the local gym. Devontae was reading in his apartment, watching after Tanisha. Nawiri was teaching Anisha how to play chess in the living room. It was a beautiful day, perhaps one of the last days they could expect to be so warm before the Fall winds blew in. Ms. Robyn went around the house saying goodbye to all of the kids and then ran outside to meet Ms. Karena.

'Hey girlfriend!' exclaimed Ms. Karena.

'Hey! How are you feeling? You know, it is such a beautiful day, maybe we should jog to the gym!'

'Sure, why not?' responded Ms. Karena. They began to jog. Lungs inflating with fresh, crisp air and arms flailing to the rhythm of their hastening breathe. Fallen sticks and curbsides served as small obstacles in their route as well as the slight incline of the street. Needless to say, after five minutes, they were each heavily fatigued and the fast jog gradually slowed to a brisk walk. 'I guess we're not as in shape as we used to be.' They both laughed.

As they neared the workout center, Ms. Karena brought up a subject that had been troubling her. 'Can I ask you a question Robyn?'

'Of course, as long as it's not about my ex-husband because I just hate to even think of him!' replied Ms. Robyn.

'Oh, no. Hell no! Girl, I like to forget I even have an ex-husband, so I completely understand. I wanted to ask you about your relationship with Nawiri. I've noticed how you all interact with each another. It's almost like she's your friend and I have no idea how to have that type of relationship with Sasha. I just don't understand her, she's so quiet, she always keeps to herself and I never know what she's thinking.'

‘Well, do you ask her?’

‘Not really, I would rather her just open up to me.’

‘So, why do you think she’s not opening up to you?’

‘I don’t know, she’s just a strange child.’

‘Hmm, so tell me what a typical day is like when she gets home from school? Does she speak? What does she say? And what do you say to her?’

‘She speaks but then she just goes to her room until I have to remind her lazy ass about her chores.’

‘Do you have to remind her or are you just assuming that she forgot?’

‘I know she does because she’s so absent-minded.’

‘Well, it sounds to me like you’re making a lot of assumptions about her character. Maybe you should try not reminding her and see if she does them anyway.’

‘Well, what about the not talking to me part?’

‘Engage her in conversation. I’m sure if you give her a chance, ask questions and be patient that she will open up. Every child has something to say. They have feelings and thoughts just like we do. Just because she’s keeping them inside doesn’t mean she’s absent-minded. Perhaps you have to change the environment to make her more comfortable.’

‘I guess. I just can’t wait for her to move out, so I can have my space and freedom back.’

‘You know what? She can probably sense that you feel that way. So, what can you expect from a child that feels unwelcomed in their own home? She’s isolating herself to protect herself. This is a two way street, you can’t expect her to open up to you without you also showing some vulnerability to her.’

‘I’ll have to think about that some more because I do want our relationship to be better. I just don’t know if I’m ready to do the type of self-evaluation that you’re talking about.’

‘I know it’s not easy because I am struggling with the same thing right now. The only reason why it appears that Nawiri and I have a good relationship is because she is a very forgiving child and because she has escaped the feeling of neglect because my mother has been raising her. So, yeah, we seem like friends because she’s more of a friend to me than a daughter. It’s a struggle for you and me both! I didn’t read any manuals on how to be a good mother or how to deal with depression or how not to let my internal struggles affect my parenting. We just have to keep supporting and uplifting each other and giving advice the best way we know how. That’s what friends are for, right?’ Ms. Robyn put her arm around Ms. Karena and kissed her on the cheek, ‘It’ll all work out, don’t worry.’ They arrived at the gym already sweating from their morning walk. They caught the attention of many men in the weight area and couldn’t help but to laugh when one of them dropped a dumb bell, distracted with awe, as they passed by. Forty was the new thirty.

In the meantime, Sasha sat with a large glass of orange juice, quietly observing the intense Chess lesson that Anisha was receiving from Nawiri. Nawiri was focused on practicing her most complicated tricks to make Anisha a more intuitive player. 'Make sure you're paying attention to the pawn structure. How recently did you count the value of the pieces?'

'I just did after my last move,' responded Anisha.

'Good, good. Hmm, ok but you left this space open. Check. Sasha, why are you so quiet? What's up girl? You know Devontae has inspired me, I think I want to start making music too, we could be a group. Me and you can be the singers and Devontae will be the MC.'

'But I can't sing,' Sasha laughed.

'Ok, then you can be another MC. You can turn some of that beautiful poetry you write into rap lyrics.'

Sasha continued to laugh, 'Girl, you are crazy, no way. I can't even imagine being on stage or even in front of that freestyle crowd at school. No way, I couldn't do it. I got too much stage fright.'

'Whatever, you never even tried, so how do you know if you have stage fright or not?'

'I just know.'

‘Ok fine, I guess it can just be me and Devontae.’

‘And have you talked to him about your idea?’

‘No, but I gotta write some stuff first to show him that I can be a valuable asset to the group.’

‘Hahaha, girl you crazy. Good luck with that. I’m interested to hear what kind of music duo you two would make. But listen, I’m about to step outside for a second, can you meet me on the back porch when you finish this game? I have something I want to talk to you about.’

‘Alright,’ Nawiri responded with a look of confusion, ‘Is everything ok?’

‘I’ll just talk to you when you get done,’ Sasha said as she exited the living room.

The game of Chess continued, Nawiri tried to move the game along as quickly as possible without rushing Anisha’s moves. Anisha was a very quick learner; she had mastered the game of Checkers in a few days and was looking for a greater challenge in the game of Chess.

‘Are you sure you want to move your Queen right there? You see where my King is?’ asked Nawiri.

‘Oh, shoot. Yeah, I do,’ said Anisha as she moved her Queen back to her original position.

The game continued for another ten minutes with Nawiri pointing out each of Anisha’s weak points and thus allowing her to win the game.

'Checkmate!' It was the first of many Chess games to come, a game that Anisha was growing to love already.

'I'm gonna step outside and talk to Sasha, you wanna go hang out in the garage with Devontae and Tanisha?'

'Naw, I think I'm going to take a shower and read this book Devontae suggested that I read.'

'Ok cool, what book is it?'

'It's called 'Roll of Thunder Hear my Cry', have you heard of it?'

'Yup, I really liked that book actually. I think you'll enjoy it too. Devontae would know, he's read like every book in my mom's library by now. Well, I guess I'll see you in a little bit.'

'Ok, see ya,' Anisha walked up the stairs and Nawiri travelled into the kitchen, poured a glass of apple juice for herself and headed outside to the backyard. Just as she emerged in the driveway, she could see Devontae coming out of his living room.

'Hey,' yelled Devontae to Sasha and Nawiri.

'Hey,' they yelled back to him.

'I just got the urge to shoot some hoops, you guys wanna play with me?' Ms. Robyn had just purchased a new basketball and basketball hoop for the kids to play with in the driveway. Prior to having a boy in the household, she had never considered buying one but with Devontae and three other children, she figured basketball would be a useful recreational activity. Sasha declined the offer but Nawiri accepted, not realizing the urgency of Sasha's request to talk.

Devontae was not a very good basketball player but he was much better than Nawiri, who could barely dribble the ball and whose aim was certainly deadly to the surrounding fences, flower patches, and vegetables gardens. In a game of one-on-one, she made weak attempts to block his shots, jumping into the air waving her hands frantically and then ducking from the ball when it was headed toward the basketball net. When it was her turn to shoot, she bounced the ball twice, or three times if she was feeling bold. Then, she travelled for 30 seconds before making a sad attempt at aiming for the backboard. Devontae was bent over laughing at Nawiri's lack of skills as Sasha shook her right foot frantically, impatiently waiting for the game to finish. It seemed to be the longest game of one-on-one basketball she had ever watched; each bounce of the ball was like a slow motion scene from the movie Love & Basketball. The flirting by way of feigned competition would have been cute to Sasha on any other occasion than this one. Devontae stole the ball, twirled around Nawiri and made a perfect shot. The wait was so painstaking for Sasha that she suddenly jumped up and screamed out Nawiri's name. She turned, alarmed by Sasha's outburst. 'I really need you to come with me, right now,' Sasha demanded in an urgent tone. They walked down the driveway, leaving Devontae in a state of bewilderment. He wasn't sure if he should follow or stay behind but quickly decided that he would rather play basketball than to participate in 'girl talk.'

They could hear two women talking as they approached the front of the house and Sasha stopped in her tracks and began to retreat backwards. Nawiri stood still observing the wide-eyed look on Sasha's face. She had never seen her best friend look so terrified in her life. Usually, she was the one standing up for the two of them in school, not afraid of conflict or fighting if necessary. When they saw that the two women talking were only neighbors, Sasha grabbed Nawiri's hand and began to run down the street.

'Come on, we have to hurry before they get back!' panted Sasha as she pulled Nawiri along.

'Where are we going? You know G'Ma is home right?'

'Yeah but she's taking a nap, I peaked in her room.'

They ran as if a vicious dog was on their tail, sniffing out their trail and hunting for the kill. Luckily for them, traffic was light through the neighborhood. Otherwise, jetting into the street at intersections could have been quite disastrous. Only a block away from their destination, Sasha took a moment to answer Nawiri's question.

'To the clinic.'

'What clinic? How close is it? I'm getting tired.'

'It's right up here on the main street, I've seen it before.'

'Why can't you just have your mom take you? I'm sorry but I have to stop, I'm too tired,' Nawiri started to walk and Sasha started to walk as well but held Nawiri's hand to make her keep up the pace.

'It's a pregnancy clinic.'

Nawiri stopped in her path. 'What do you mean, pregnancy clinic?'

'I think I'm pregnant Nawiri and I'm scared, so I want you to come with me.' Sasha hurried along, taking long strides.

'But how can you be pregnant?'

'Because I had sex and I missed my period last month.'

'But when did you have sex? You never told me!' She began to jog to catch up with Sasha, who had not stopped walking.

'It's been a long time now. I think it started when I was ten. My mom's ex-boyfriend, Maurice, liked to play 'house' with me, where he was the Daddy and I was the Mommy. Ever since then, I couldn't stop. It's like I can't control it. But I actually like Brandon, so I didn't make him use a condom and I think I might be pregnant now,' Sasha face was hot with tears. She had never opened up to anyone about these things; she even hid her secrets from herself by trying to forget them day after day.

'I don't understand. Why didn't you ever tell me this? It's like you are living two lives.' Nawiri was in a state of shock.

'Because I knew you wouldn't understand but now, I have no choice. I can't do this by myself,' Sasha cried.

They arrived at New Hope Clinic and were greeted by a receptionist who looked at them both skeptically but still gave Sasha the paperwork to fill out for a walk-in appointment. They waited in the lobby for fifteen minutes before a doctor called Sasha into her office. It was an awkward wait with other teens glancing around, making eye contact and giving small smiles of understanding before they went back to staring at the floor. They were all searching for the same comfort as they were all there for abortions or something else related to sexual health. You could see the desperation in their faces, hoping that they could go on living normal childhoods even with dark secrets to carry with them. The trauma of pregnancy soon to be followed by the trauma of abortion left them stunned in silence. Sasha wondered what her baby would have looked like; maybe it would have had her nose and Brandon's eyes, or her ears and Brandon's dimples, or his long legs and her honey brown complexion. She could see a vague outline of a face in her daydream but there was no one around it, only a few toys. It seemed lonely. These thoughts were very disturbing to her; so she began to drown out the fear of giving birth to a lonely baby with Aaliyah's lyrics and Timberland beats. Humming as the doctor peered down at her as if she was a lost puppy. 'Hello, Sasha. Are you sure you've come to the right place today? Are you aware of what we do here?' The doctor asked with a thick accent.

'Yes, I believe I have. I would like to take a pregnancy test and if I test positive, then I want an abortion.'

'Do your parents know about this?'

'No, my mother cannot find out. She already hates me; she will kill me if she finds out. Please, I understand what I'm doing. I just turned fifteen, so there is no way that I am telling my mother. I would rather die than to face her with this.'

The doctor looked very perturbed. 'Well, let us just see what the test results show. Follow the instructions on the package and bring it back to me when you're finished in the bathroom.' She showed Sasha to the bathroom and went to speak with another clinician about her ethical dilemma.

The clinic had the smell of sterile instruments and latex gloves. To avoid feeling nauseous, she breathed through her mouth. Sasha didn't dare to look at the stick she held in her hand, she just took it straight to the doctor and closed her eyes tight, anticipating the news. Streams of tears flowed from her eyes when she heard the results. She hugged the doctor tight, to prevent herself from falling onto the hard, cold floor. The results read negative. The doctor explained that sometimes, women miss their periods due to various stress factors in their lives and that Sasha should see her regular physician if she missed another month.

'But even though you are clear for pregnancy. I'd like to do a cervical swab to make sure you have not contracted any sexually transmitted diseases. It is not my job to tell you what to do my darling but you are a beautiful young girl and if you were my daughter, I would tell you to be extremely careful because even the finest boy could have a disease and pass it on to you. And depending on the disease, it could affect your health for the rest of your life. Here, let me give you this pamphlet. It talks about all of the different types of STDs and their symptoms. You can go ahead and wait in the lobby for another ten minutes and I will call you back to hear the results of the test.'

Sasha walked into the lobby, smiling from ear-to-ear. Nawiri knew that she must have received good news, so she stood to give Sasha a hug. They embraced one another for what seemed like hours before taking their seats again. Sasha looked at the pictures in the pamphlet that the doctor had given her and she became even more scared of STDs than the prospect of having a baby. They each began to worry about the time. Their mothers would surely not work out for more than two hours nor would her grandmother need that long of a nap and it was approaching the two hour mark. The doctor came back into the lobby and called Sasha into her office. 'Well, it looks like you do have an STD, it's called Chlamydia. Luckily for you, it is in its early stages and once we get you on some medication, you shouldn't have any ongoing problems. But Please, Please, Please my dear, use protection in the future. I can't tell you not to have sex, even though you are very young to be engaging in such activities, but since you are, just be careful. You see now that there are serious health consequences to irresponsible sexual behavior.' 'Yes Ma'am,' responded the fearful young girl in front of her. She sent Sasha along with a prescription slip for the local pharmacy. The visit had cost Sasha all of her hard earned money from her summer job.

Walking back into the lobby, she caught eyes with Nawiri. As if they had read one another's minds, they rushed out of the front door of the clinic and ran through the neighborhood, taking shortcuts wherever possible, trying to beat time. Running through backyards, unskillfully hopping fences, one of which had edges so jagged that Nawiri's pant leg tore from a seam near the knee down to the ankle. Making their way back onto Ashton Avenue and cutting diagonally across to Gloucester Drive, they neared the house but their efforts were in vain. Ms. Karena and Ms. Robyn had been there for twenty minutes interrogating Devontae as to where Nawiri and Sasha had disappeared to.

Before they could make up an explanation, Ms. Karena was already storming down the driveway to meet Sasha. By her facial expression, they knew she was about to go off. Towering over her, she yelled, 'Where the fuck have you been? Did I tell you, you could leave the house? You think you grown Miss Thang?'

'No,' responded Sasha weakly. Ms. Robyn, Nawiri, Devontae, and Anisha looked on, in shock. None of them had ever seen Ms. Karena in the type of rage that she was in, an occurrence that Sasha witnessed and endured every day.

'Shut up!' Ms. Karena slapped Sasha across the face, bringing her small frame to the ground. Ms. Robyn moved to interfere but Ms. Karena looked at her with a gaze so fierce and intimidating that she decided to stay back. She ordered Sasha to get into the car and she drove away without saying goodbye to anyone. Sasha leaned against the car door, flinching at the sound of her mother's high-pitched screams. She could finally see the first lines of her contest entry – *Mirror mirror on the wall, who's the fairest of them all? But the mirror had no time to respond because she shattered it with her powerful fist and devoured the glass that shone brightly on the floor. Destroying her internal and external image without mercy. My mother is a beauty queen turned monster.*

I KEEP

Part 1

Devontae placed his world encyclopedia aside. The essay contest had begun to weigh on his mind. A story, his life. His life in the form of a story? It just seemed like an impossible task. He and Sasha had discussed potential topics but it was not until he had a frightening dream about losing one of his sisters forever that he decided to write about their impeccable resilience. Every day, Cambria, Anisha and Tanisha inspired him to be the best that he could possibly be. They were not perfect but one thing they did do – especially well – was keep on smiling even through the toughest of times. And he was the brother, the man, the bread winner, the keeper of peace, the reasonable magician, responsible for bringing logic into the illogical world of women, the protector, the sword and the shield. But Cambria's strong will and determination always seemed to outshine the role he envisioned for himself as she was the one who kept the family together and out of the foster care system.

How does one summarize his life-long thoughts and feelings, disappointments and triumphs into one simple essay? Fourteen – almost fifteen – short years on the planet Earth felt like a hundred to

Devontae with heightened levels of stress to mark each passing year. He laid his head back; the top of the couch cushion conforming to the shape of his neck. His father had left, unexpectedly, when he was three. That had been the first shock to his innocent psyche; so vividly could he remember the feeling of his father's presence compared to the empty backdrop that remained in his absence. Many people began to disappear after his father, first his grandmother, and eventually playmates and friends. Their bodies dropping like flies and spirits ascending, dispersing themselves through the atmosphere. Evening swept upon him as he sifted through bittersweet memories. There was a knock at the door and when he went to open it, he found Nawiri dressed in dark blue jeans and a white t-shirt with a black hoodie on top. Her simple attire spoke volumes to him. He loved it. 'Hey you, I just made some sun tea and I brought you a glass,' she said as she stepped into the living room. She set the glass on the cocktail table and took a seat on the opposite end of the couch. So, what have you been doing all day? I think my mom and I are about to go to the market to get some flowers for the vases in the house. She is really trying to be involved these days. Usually it's me and my G'Ma doing everything together. It's nice having her back around, I've been missing her for a long time now. You wanna come?' Devontae was amused as usual, 'Do you really think I want to go buy flowers?' He laughed and then straightened up when he saw the serious look on Nawiri's face, 'I don't know that's why I asked.'

'Oh, well, maybe next time, I have a few things I wanted to get done. I've just been reading and I was about to start working on this writing contest. What is sun tea by the way?'

'It's regular tea but I put it in the sun and the herbal flavor diffused through the water all day. Then, I added honey and lemon and ice, so it's perfect now. What writing contest? I wanna enter.'

'Aww dang, I meant to tell you before. It's um, private, kind of, if that makes any sense.'

'No, it doesn't make sense. I've never heard of a private contest. Shouldn't anyone be able to enter?'

'Well, they selected a group of people that can participate and out of that group, there will be ten winners. Honestly, I think they chose people who they think need the money because there were a lot of people who weren't there that I would have expected to be there.'

'What?! This is discrimination!'

'But Nawiri, you can afford to go to this private high school if you want to go and we can't, so they're trying to give us a chance. It's like eliminating a financial disparity.'

'But it's not my fault that...' She paused, thinking of how insensitive the rest of her statement might sound to him.

'That what? That I'm poor? No, it's not your fault but you don't lose anything if someone else wins the scholarship.'

'But they could be taking my spot.'

'Well, I'm sure that if you are a good student, which I know you are, then you won't have any trouble getting into any high school. You gotta try seeing things from other people's perspectives sometimes. It's not like other people are always right but if you could just imagine what it is like to be in someone else's shoes, then maybe you could understand them and their struggles better.'

'Well, good luck with your contest but I didn't come up here to get a lecture. So, I'm gonna go now. We're leaving at six o' clock if you change your mind.'

'Alright, and I'm sorry if it sounded like a lecture. I wasn't trying to lecture you but just think about it. How else am I supposed to afford private school? Can I have a hug?'

'Sure,' she said, slumping her shoulders and looking defeated. 'Don't look so sad, there are so many other scholarships and contests you can apply to.' He had grown over the summer, so he towered over her 5'4" stature with his 5'8" frame and embraced her affectionately. Nawiri walked away smiling, his hugs always brightened up her day. She turned to go and he grabbed her wrist, she turned back to face him and asked, 'What?' Devontae responded, 'Nothing, I just wanted to see you smile again.' Nawiri blushed and hurried down the stairs. Devontae went back to the couch and laid down in the exact same spot.

The process was draining from writing down specific memories and examples of his family's resilience to piecing the puzzle together. He had never felt so enlivened by an assignment from school. Usually, the work was mundane and irrelevant to his everyday life but this – this was a test of his ability to express his deepest emotions – fear, joy, and sadness. He went to the table and opened his notebook, example one was when Cambria lit candles one winter because the electricity was out and made dinner in the dark, then checked homework and told bedtime stories until everyone was asleep. He could also remember countless times when Anisha would help Tanisha get dressed, eat, clean herself up, explain cartoon plots, and even listen to her talk when it made no sense to anyone at all. And unlike most autistic children, Tanisha had stayed fairly calm throughout the entire moving process from the projects to the Heath/Simmons mansion. The more he thought about his sisters, the more he wondered where Cambria was, 'That girl is too much. She's probably in another state by now. She was always so restless. Don't want nobody telling her what to do. I swear if I see Red again, I'm gonna kill him. Naw, I'm not. Who am I kidding? But that nigga ain't shit, he probably keepin' my sister hostage. Who knows what his old ass is up to. Cambria, sis, please be careful out there. I hope I'll see you again someday. I still can't believe she's not here. Shit is too crazy.' Devontae decided to focus on the paper, he stared down at the intimidating white sheet. It was perfect – no scratches, no rips, no folds, no smudges. He didn't want to touch the paper with his pen, afraid to taint the fresh, crispness of it. He placed his pen to the paper and let a small black drop bleed onto the sheet. Now that the sheet was no longer so empty, he began to write fluidly.

In the beginning, we were a happy family. I wasn't aware of what I didn't have because I had never seen more. My mother tended to our needs, provided food, showed us love and hid her secrets well. But life has a way of testing our limits, pushing us into situations where we don't know what to do, and challenging us to step outside of our boundaries. Many are not comfortable with such challenges but some laugh in the face of adversity and are excited to show their limitless potential. Three such young women happen to be my sisters.

As long as my sisters are alive, I will see to it personally that they thrive in this world. Sometimes we wonder why life can be so unfortunate to some and so good to others. I have come to the conclusion that I must not allow my circumstances to dictate my mindset. My sister, Cambria, always used to say that 'we didn't ask for this life but while we're here, we have to be strong, there's no other choice.' But I disagree, we do have a choice. I could choose to be weak, to let my circumstances defeat me, to wither under ceaseless pressure and crumble like a brick of charcoal. I could choose to let my feelings and emotions guide my actions. I could choose to feel pain. But my sisters have repeatedly shown me that when you choose strength, every day is not only bearable but enjoyable but when you choose despair it's like choosing to exist amongst the living dead and that is something I do not want to be a part of.

A few years ago, a man broke into our home and tried to rob us. We weren't really scared because we didn't have much for him to take but it was the shock of having an intruder standing inside of our comfort zone that scared us the most. To ease the tension, my sisters actually began to load up bags full of toys and different things lying around the house. They were so helpful to the robber that by the time they had finished collecting almost everything we owned for this stranger, this filthy intruder, he couldn't even take it. He felt too guilty and went right back out of the window he came in, embarrassed and ashamed, apologizing profusely. Security was a foreign concept to us, reinforced by our safety being in constant jeopardy. Furthermore, we felt dejected and angry because both our parents and our grandparents had not been there to protect us. But because we had each other's love, a real but unspoken love, we were able to survive these challenging, parentless nights. It was an infectious and contagious love; everybody wanted some. Neighbors and strangers alike came to the door just to experience it and the love seeped out of the house through the front door and even through the walls. Bled into the streets, soaked the concrete and was absorbed by the grass and even the weeds, attracting the most gracious folk and the most contemptible ones. The love outshined our imperfections and we could live with ourselves. We even went as far as to enjoy life and to cherish the smallest things, choosing to ignore the more blatant misconstructions, misunderstandings, mishaps and missing people. The holes that pierced our hearts were filled in with stones and rocks but we hid it well from ourselves and from each other.

Looking to the future, I don't know exactly what I want to be. Sometimes I want to be an astronaut, sometimes a philosopher and sometimes a politician. It varies because my interests change as I learn about the world – history, people, politics, nature, the economy, science – all fascinate me. I soak in information to enhance my perspective and I believe that Andover High School is the best place for me to continue my search for knowledge and understanding. It would also place me on a trajectory toward a career that would allow me to provide a secure and comfortable life for my mother and three beautiful sisters. There was a time when I doubted happiness but now I know that happiness is constantly available, I only have to claim it as mine. I choose strength, I choose life and I choose love.

Part 2

Embarrassment could have been the word to describe Sasha's feelings after her mother so eloquently humiliated her in front of her friends but the hatred, erupting like a volcano in her mind, had demolished all of her other emotions. There was an aura of grief in the household as something very precious seemed to have been lost in that moment in the driveway. Perhaps it was Ms. Karena's last ounce of respect for Sasha or Sasha's last inkling of love for her mother. Maybe it was a bit of both. Like a thick cloud covering the eye's cornea, they walked about the house in a daze, blinded by hatred.

Sasha sat down to write her story but writer's block had grabbed hold of her creative consciousness. She could not decide if she wanted the composition to be a long poem or an essay; serious or playful; melancholy or joyful. Poetry was her niche but an essay would allow her to expand on things without having to worry about the mechanics of a poem. Serious was who she was but perhaps playful would grab the attention of the judges. Meloncholy was how she felt but no judge likes to feel depressed after reading an entry. In the end, she decided to go with a positive poem about the healing power of friendship, specifically her friendship with Nawiri. Writing about her life was already a bountiful leap outside of her comfort zone but she was determined to meet the challenge. Tired of being an annoying failure in her mother's eyes and even more ready to pack up and ship off to a free boarding school, she began to write.

Mirror mirror on the wall, who's the fairest of them all?

But the mirror had no time to respond, she shattered it with her powerful fist

Bending and collapsing her weakened wrist, it was the joint that supported the fist

Arthritis and depression hit, she threw repeated, convulsive fits

Self-destruction was her middle name, she'd missed the opportunity for fortune and fame

Thought life could never possibly be the same, with bills, dishes and three kids calling her name

She was a nightmare, a feign, a hyena, a predator, a nightstalker, a werewolf, a tornado

She plundered down the darkest path, grabbing passersby but I found a way to escape though

I held on to relationships that helped me foster growth when the going got rough

'Nah, this is too negative. I need to start a little bit more upbeat. I probably shouldn't talk about Momma at all,' Sasha thought to herself. She put her pen to the paper and tried again.

This is an official appeal to the admissions committee

City girl, honor student, nappy hair, plus I'm witty

Honestly, you need me to fill your quota for diversity

I'll probably fly through the basketball ranks straight to varsity

Bring publicity and money, you'll never want me to leave

'No, wait. Scratch that, they would never like this. Argh!' Sasha put her forehead in the palms of her hands, trying to think of the best way to start the poem. Third try:

I was a hop and a skip away from jumping off of the Ambassador Bridge

A lonely, misunderstood, low self-confidence kid

Lost and confused in a world too big

Amazed by all of the shiny cars, rings, stars and things

I worshipped them to hide the pain and the empty feelings

Indoors, outdoors, upstairs, downstairs, they were all the same

But friendship saved my life in many ways on those cold, rainy days

When the going got tough, my best friend would say

'I got the anecdote, I got the solution;

I'll love you til' the end of time, no need for temporary resolutions.'

We eat together, talk together, think together,

Now I'm at ease, feeling about myself much better

The power of friendship can go so far

Enabling or disabling, whichever you allow

I hit home runs in my sleep, wake up and repeat the same things

Dreams becoming realities because I believe in me

My past is inconsequential, when I realize the value I bring

A unique perspective of city life, like a cracked bell with a valiant ring

Nothing but potential is what I think of as the future

I love expression, healthy food and cutting down on the sucre

Not quite ready to become a vegetarian

But I am ready to be an Andover student, an artist, a poet and even a veterinarian

To the educational table, I bring diversity of thought

Books, journals, magazines, you name it, I've bought

A dusty foot philosopher, excited to explore the world

Instead of seeking artifacts, diamonds and pearls

I'm more keen to conversation and hanging with my girl

The one who inspired me to keep pushing through negativity

To hold my head up and to be proud of being me

And eventually the potential in me, we won't be the only ones to see

I hope, every day, that she was right about these things

Being chosen to apply for this scholarship was sort of an affirmation

Now, I feel like I can accomplish anything with a little determination

With your rigorous program and my relentless drive

There is no goal for which I cannot strive

I like to ride my bike, roller skate and write poetry

To think about poverty, suffering and the world's inequalities

I am excited about Andover's sports, music and creative writing programs

And in your production studio, on my musical and lyrical talents, I could expand

Exploring the endless opportunities on your campus

Will surely prepare me for higher education or any vocational school

In an environment where knowledge is the prize and my mind is the tool

There are no limitations, no ceilings over my head

When discouraging words are spoken, I choose to ignore them instead

I stay humble and thankful for my essential daily bread

My motto is resilience and my favorite color is red

Many people will come to know me in the school, despite its large size

Because of my work ethic, my expansive love and my passion for life

Proofreading. Editing. Sharing. Discussing. Devontae and Sasha swapped papers to get one another's opinions. The deadline was approaching and every applicant was nervous with anticipation. Quivering as they turned in the final drafts of their entries, they looked to the teachers for nods or smiles of reassurance. After they turned in their essays, short stories, poems and other forms of media through which they had answered the prompt, the wait began. The slowly passing time was agonizing; it would be six long months before the announcement of the winners at the Spring Concert in May. In December, each applicant received a notification in the mail, verifying that their entry had been received by the school faculty decision board. In January, there was nothing but snow, dreary skies, early mornings and dreadful homework. February brought more ski trips, museum visits and school projects that kept them too busy to think about the contest. In March, they prepared for the placement exam that would qualify them for the three best public schools in the city. And spring brought a warm buzz of excitement in April. Longer days and outdoor lunch periods were the biggest distraction of all. Both the contest and the school work were temporarily put on hold for the games that ensued on the playground.

May came quicker than they had expected. Each teacher was preparing their class for the assembly in the gymnasium. The morning clouds had just cleared and the children seemed to have more energy as the sun fought its way through. There were many side conversations taking place as Ms. Johnson tried to get the attention of her ninth grade science class.

'Excuse me students, excuse me! You need to listen or else we will stay here and not go to the concert.'

Most students had not heard her threats as there was much chatter coming from every corner of the classroom. Andrew was playing in Sasha's long, silky hair. Some of the dolls were arguing amongst themselves. Apparently, one of them had just started her period and told another one, who went on to misconstrue the story and accidentally told another one that the first girl was pregnant when she really wasn't. So, the third doll asked the first if it was true and the first was upset that her confidant had lied and proceeded to call her a 'bitch,' a statement in which the third doll gladly passed on to the second. And so, this was the conversation between all nine of them that was meant to clear the air but had brought out many other unexpected secrets, lies and scandals. The conversation was escalating into an emotional argument when Ms. Johnson began to bang a ruler against the table.

'Attention!! Attention!! Attention!!' she yelled.

The chatter halted as everyone turned around to see the beet red face of their teacher.

'Now, if I hear another word out of anyone, they will be going straight to the office! This is not a zoo! This is MY classroom and you WILL show some respect! Anyone who is in band or choir, you may go join them. Everyone else, quietly get up and make your way to the gym, our class will be sitting on the right hand side near the stage. If I see anyone wandering, you will have an AUTOMATIC detention! You are dismissed.'

The students began to make their way down the hallway, continuing their disrupted conversations. Anthony Roberts began to pick on Steven Jones. 'Man, you stank. You don't have no shower at yo' house dawg?' He and his friends laughed. Steven ignored him. 'I guess not, this nigga can't even speak up and defend himself. A dirty, mute nigga.'

'Shut up! Leave me alone!' shouted Steven. He quickened his pace to catch up with Ms. Johnson and to avoid the chastisement. Meanwhile, Devontae was busy discussing his top picks for the NBA finals, with some of the boys who he was betting against. Nawiri listened vaguely, trying to familiarize herself with the names of the teams and players so that she wouldn't be completely clueless when Devontae would attempt after school to discuss it with her, as if she had any interest but Sasha stole away her attention with a new story about how she suspected that Brandon was cheating on her again and wanted advice on what she should do and if she should still invite him to Junior

Prom. 'I may just go with Andrew,' Sasha whispered, 'I think he might like me, did you see the way he was playing in my hair?' Nawiri nodded her head yes. 'I did. So, what are you gonna say?' Sasha shrugged her shoulders, 'I don't know, nothing, I guess. I gotta wait for him to come ask me.'

The gymnasium was packed, every class was present. Sasha and Nawiri rushed to the bleachers to get seats next to their other friends. It was always nice to sit by friends, it made the assemblies much more enjoyable, no one really understood why, perhaps it was just the special feeling that came with their surrounding presence and funny side comments throughout the event.

To the right of Nawiri, Thomas and Henry were cracking jokes on one another's skin tone, 'Man, I almost couldn't find you last night, which yo' ol' black concrete looking self.'

'Dawg, forget you, which yo' ol' yellow, head lights lookin' self.'

'Nigga, you need head lights to illuminate yo' ol' Doo doo brown turd lookin' face.'

'O, it's like that! I'll shit on yo' ol' macaroni and cheese crayola crayon lookin' ass.'

The boys went on and on until Sasha yelled at them. 'Would ya'll shut up! Damn! What is the point of trying to make each feel bad about your skin complexions? You sound like idiots!'

They looked at her, surprised at the outburst. 'We were just playin' around, dang Sasha,' responded Henry, defensively. He had always had a secret crush on her and was disappointed that the one time she spoke to him was when she was upset with him. 'Well, maybe ya'll should 'play' nicer. You over there making ME feel self-conscious!'

'Dang, I'm sorry, I didn't mean to,' said Henry, ashamed. Thomas remained silent, irritated by Sasha's interjection, 'I wasn't even talking to her,' he mumbled.

The program began. The first group to perform was the C band, then the B band and then the A band. The choir went after them. Sasha, Devontae and the other Andover High School scholarship participants sat holding their breath every time a group walked off of the stage, expecting the principal to emerge and announce the winners. But each time they were disappointed. After the choir sang a beautiful rendition of the Black National Anthem, the African Dance troup performed, followed by solo poets, singers and lyricists. Finally, the school drama group acted out a series of short skits. And then, at exactly 3:30pm, as the last bell of the day was ringing. Mr. Edison walked to the center of the stage and began to speak.

'Before you all are dismissed for the day, I would like to announce that out of the ten Andover High School tuition scholarships awarded this year to students around the city, three of them are designated for three outstanding Century Academy students. When, I call your name would you please join me on the stage?'

Devontae looked down the row at Nawiri. She smiled and winked optimistically; she had gotten over her jealousy and was excited for the possibility of her two best friends winning such a prestigious award.

'Our first awardee is Andrew Jackson, please hold your applause until all three names are called.'

But the students couldn't help themselves; everyone loved Andrew and his creative style, so they cheered him on as he made his way to the stage. 'Our next awardee is none other than Ms. Sashaaaaa Gordon!' The crowd burst into applause again. Devontae held his breathe and looked down. 'And last but most definitely not least, the third winner from Century Academy of the Andover High School full tuition award, the most prestigious private high school in the state is drum roll please!' Everyone pounded on the bleachers, 'Devontae Harris!' Devontae looked up, with a look of shock, his heart skipped a beat when he heard his name. The crowd was roaring with cheers and applause and those around him moved away to give him room to climb down from the bleachers. Sasha, Devontae and Andrew stood on the stage, gazing out over their counterparts. It was such an exhilarating moment for the three of them that they seemed to be frozen, not knowing whether to keep smiling or to face one another or the crowd. They swayed, awkwardly, until directed to take their seats. Devontae spotted Nawiri; she was smiling harder than he was, a genuine look of pride shown through her eyes and uplifted his spirits to an even higher level of jubilation. Sasha thought that Nawiri was looking at her, so she smiled back, feeling so lucky to have such a supportive best friend.

Nawiri was, in fact, looking at both of them, oblivious to the significance of her radiant smile.

READY FOR LOVE

Part 1

The school year was flying by like the speed of light. They had enjoyed the Fall, endured the Winter, and had now emerged into a disappointingly chilly Spring. Sasha and Devontae were still floating on air from winning the Andover High School scholarship. They still had a few weeks to make a decision about whether or not they were going to accept the scholarship or split with the money. After visiting the school, Devontae realized why the scholarship existed.

Only about ten percent of the student population identified themselves as minorities, and only five percent were African American. Unlike their middle school where the kids talked to, argued with, laughed with and made fun of one another in the classrooms, in the hallway, outside of the school, in the bathroom, on the playground, during student assemblies, and on field trips, everyone at Andover seemed so quiet and disciplined. Their lips were pierced tight as they listened intently to every syllable that came out of the mouths of their teachers. It was as if the class was bound by a quiet spell. Devontae was impressed that students were so respectful but fell bored and was missing the constant commotion of Century. He, Sasha and Nawiri ate lunch with the black students at Andover and marveled at their speech and their strange inflections. It was still English but every word had a special twang; they put emphasis on 'A' and 'E' more than any other letters. Devontae walked away to use the restroom, the unfamiliarity was beginning to overwhelm him. During the second half of the day, classes were a little livelier, as they were able to attend a band class and participate in some hands-on science experiments.

They left the school with mixed feelings about the institution. On one hand, it was a great place for learning, with less distractions, more resources, smaller classes and state of the art facilities. But on the other hand, they missed the culture of their community and wondered if they would lose touch with their friends back at home. It was a tough decision to make.

'Hey Sasha wait up!' Devontae jogged up to her, in the hallway.

'What's up D?'

'Nothin' much, chillin'. But I just wanted to ask you if you made a decision?'

'About what?'

'About Andover.'

'Oh, naw. I thought we were gonna make a decision together. All three of us.'

'O, ok. Well, ain't nobody talkin' about it, so I just figured ya'll were making your minds up, individually. But I been thinkin' about it hard and honestly, I just can't see myself there. I mean it seems like a great school, don't get me wrong, but damn. Those kids are like zombies.

I'ma be bored as hell or even worse, I'll become like them. I just don't think I can do it.'

'Hmm, I see where you're coming from but I guess, I look at it as a chance to get away from all this craziness in the city, you feel me? It doesn't need to be action all the time. Half the time, I be ready to slap somebody's child in class for talking in my ear and distracting me from learning. I'm gonna take the scholarship. So, what school do you want to go to?'

'Renaissance, it's the best public high school in the city. And we all got in, so I figured that would be the next best thing. Then, we can save the money and use it for college, you know?'

'True, well I know you are going to be a beast anywhere you go as long as you stay outta these streets! Have you talked to Nawiri about this? You know her mom is probably going to make her go to Andover or some other private school.'

'Naw, she ain't talkin' to me, I think she's mad at me,' he laughed.

'Yeah, she is actually. Why are you laughing? God, you can be such an asshole.'

'Because I know why she's mad but she won't be so mad when she sees what I have planned.'

'Ok, so if you know so much, why is she mad?'

'Can you keep a secret?'

‘Like nobody you ever knew!’ exclaimed Sasha.

‘Alright, so you already know that she’s mad because I haven’t asked her to be my Junior prom date and it’s next week.’

‘Yeah, I know.’

‘Well, I mailed the damn question last week and it’s taking forever, so if it doesn’t get to the house by this Saturday, then I’m going to just kneel down at the dinner table, like I’m proposing and just ask her in front of the whole fam.’

‘Wait, what did you put in the mail? I’m confused.’

‘I mailed the question – Will you go to Junior prom with me? – to the house with a box to check YES and a box to check NO but it’s taking way longer than I thought it would. I thought it would only take a few days but it’s been a whole week and everyday her attitude gets worse.’

Sasha laughed, ‘That’s cute, good luck with that. I’m sure one of you will let me know if or when it finally gets to the house. But I gotta run, my mom is here to pick me up early for a dentist appointment.’

‘Alright, see you later.’

‘See ya,’ Sasha ran out of the school, afraid to keep her mom waiting for too long. Sasha had been much more quiet and secretive lately because of the birth control and Chlamydia medication she was hiding, which had made Ms. Karena even more agitated than usual.

‘Hey momma,’ said Sasha lightly as she placed her book bag on the back seat.

‘Hey baby.’

Sasha looked at her, surprised that she had not begun to fuss about waiting for more than five minutes.

‘I want to stop at the park before we go to the dentist office,’ said Ms. Karena, nervously. The palms of her hands were moist with perspiration. She rubbed them on her pants leg. Then, let the window down and took deep breaths to calm her nerves. Sasha sat quietly, determined not to make, what seemed like a hot flash, any worse than it already was. They pulled up at the park, it was the warmest and most pleasant day they had seen in a long time.

‘Come on, let’s go sit on that bench over there,’ said Ms. Karena. Sasha was tempted to ask why but concealed her curiosity. On the bench, she wanted to shrivel or merely disappear under her mother’s strangely affectionate and sorrowful gaze. She had no words to describe the disdain and indifference that she had developed toward her mother. She looked at her and didn’t see a human being. She saw something that walked and talked like a human but was convinced that she was truly an alien or maybe even a demon sent from the depths of hell to torture her innocent soul. She winced when her mother’s lips parted to speak.

‘Sasha, you look so scared when I speak to you. Not even just scared but there’s an emptiness in your eyes. I don’t know what I’ve done to make you so removed.' Upon hearing this comment, Sasha burst into tears. Years of verbal abuse flooded her ears. She could hear every insult, every accusation, every curse, every word read to her out of one of her 'private' journals. They were not tears of sadness but more of rage and helplessness. Struggling to breathe, she moved away when her mother reached out a hand to console her daughter. Sasha began to shiver on an 70° day, the shoddy bench shook from her vibrations as well. The reverberations seeped into Ms. Karena's soul and she let out a loud yelp, throwing her hands up into the air and bringing them back to her face to hide the tears. They splayed and stained her silk blouse. She couldn't bring herself to look at Sasha again, so she raised her head and turned it in the opposite direction. Taking another deep breath, she began to speak, 'Ok, ok, that was a lie. I do know what I've done. I just don't know how to fix it! The damage I've done that is. I don't know how to gain your trust or your love again. Or your forgiveness. I guess I could ask but I know it's not that easy. So, I guess I just want to start by saying, I'm sorry,' she paused to take another deep breath and continued, still looking off into the distance, 'I'm sorry for everything. I never mean to say the things that I say, they just slip out of my mouth and then I think about it later and I feel bad but I can never bring myself to apologize. I mean, my father never said sorry to us, so I didn't think it was a parents place to say sorry or to even listen to their kids for that matter.'

She looked at Sasha, who was in a state of shock, still waiting for the catch line.

'Yesterday, I thought about how I would feel if someone said to me the things I say to you and how they would make me feel and I began to feel angry, more than angry, infuriated. And then, I finally realized what type of anguish you must be holding in. I guess I never considered your feelings real or important but I hear the things you say to your friends and I see the way Nawiri communicates with Ms. Heath and Ms. Robyn and now I see. I see baby and I understand that our relationship will never be healthy if I don't change. So, what do you think? Do you think I can do it?'

Sasha wrinkled her eyebrows, frowning, she responded, 'I don't know.'

'Of course, of course you don't. Hell, I don't even know. But I just wanted to tell you that I'm going to try. I'm going to go to counseling too, so that I can work out some stuff that I've been holding onto for a long time and I think that has a lot to do with the hurtful words that come out when I'm talking to you. But I don't mean it, I really don't. I know it may be hard to believe but I really do think you are beautiful, intelligent, respectful, and loving and I know in my heart that you are going to contribute greatly to this world. There's no doubt in my mind even though my words and actions hardly ever reflect it. It's the truth.'

Sasha rolled her eyes, it was the first time she had ever heard such a reaffirming positive speech from her mother but she didn't trust it.

'So, are you gonna say something?'

'What do you want me to say? You think I'm just gonna forgive you because you said sorry? We'll see if you stay true to your word. I appreciate that you finally did some self-assessment but that doesn't excuse the fifteen years of you being a bitch toward me. Well, maybe not fifteen, I would hope that you weren't trying to tear me down when I was in the crib.'

Ms. Karena smiled, it wasn't quite the response she was looking for but it was the most Sasha had said to her in a long, long time. 'It's not going to be easy. I might not be perfect but from now on I got your feelings in mind and I'm gonna try to respect you just like I would any other person. Don't think you can just run around calling me a bitch all the time 'cause I'm still your momma but I suppose I earned that title. But starting today, I'm working towards something different,' she paused, 'Anyway, you ready for this dentist appointment?'

'Yeah, sure.'

'Ok cool, let's get out of here. There are too many bugs out here anyway,' said Ms. Karena as she smacked a mosquito on her arm. Only time would tell if she could keep her promises to Sasha.

Part 2

'So, I guess he think he is too fine to go to the dance with me. Well, who the hell is he gonna go with? I know he is not gonna invite her to my house! O no, I will rip that dress right off of her…or maybe Sasha will. Anyway, I just can't believe him. All that stuff he said in the library, all those starry-eyed looks he be giving me. And for what? He can't be my man and he can't be my date, so what is the purpose of even having feelings for somebody if you can't act on them? Or even worse, what is the point of expressing those feelings and then not act on them? He's supposed to be my friend but he's steady playing with my emotions. How can somebody be so selfish? Sasha got a date, everybody's got a date, except for me! Maybe he's not going. I should ask him but no, no I shouldn't because he needs to ask me. Oh my God, he's probably out there in the garage thinkin' about anything but me. Argh, why am I so fixated with him? Get over it Nawiri, he doesn't want you! Besides, he's just a kid, I need Sasha to have her man hook me up with one of his high school friends. Yes! That would be perfect. What am I thinking? She broke up with him. Hmm, what is this? I got mail? No way, I never get mail. No return address, that's weird. Nice handwriting. What's up with all these folds. This must be some kind of joke.'

Nawiri dropped the paper that read, 'Will you go to the Junior Prom with me?' signed by Devontae Harris. Her jaw fell open as she tried to erase all of the negative thoughts that had been pervading her mind for the past two weeks. She sprinted out of the side door, across the driveway, up the garage stairs and burst through the door without knocking. Devontae was sitting on the couch reading 'Amistad' when she entered. He looked up, startled by her sudden appearance. Before he could stand, she had already run over to him and jumped into his arms kissing him all over his face. His eyelids, forehead, nose, cheeks, lips, even his neck were being showered with kisses. He wanted to kiss her back but he couldn't keep up with the position of her lips, as she was moving so fast, so he just sat back and laughed as her lips continued to travel over his face. Finally, she came back to his mouth and their lips locked securely and perfectly. Nawiri had always thought tongue kissing to be a strange and awkward kiss but she let his tongue glide into her mouth and reluctantly let hers glide into his. He turned her around, so that she could sit on the couch as he supported her back with one hand and let the other rest on the upper couch cushion. After what seemed like eternity, he sat up from their long, passionate kiss and asked, 'So, what do you say? Yes or no?'

'What do you think?' asked Nawiri.

'I just want to make sure we're on the same page.'

'Yes, of course I'll be your date.'

'Ok good, cause my tie and shoes just happen to match your dress. It would have looked kind of funny if we rode there together matching but weren't each other's dates.'

Nawiri laughed, 'So sneaky. You weren't even supposed to see my dress yet.'

'I haven't seen it, your mom told me.'

'Ahh, I see. So everybody is walking around keeping secrets from me.'

'Pretty much!'

'Ah, I hate you!' Nawiri began to tickle Devontae because she knew how ticklish he was and how much he hated to be tickled. He laughed in agony and ran out of the apartment. Nawiri chased him down the street, laughing. The buds on the trees had finally opened and the enormous branches bowed over them, creating an atmosphere similar to that of a rainforest. Nature's energy enclosed around them and propelled them forward. As they traveled farther away from the house, Ms. Heath looked after them from the front porch steps and reminisced on the days when she played with her first love. Basketball, hide-and-go-seek, tag, spin the bottle, truth or dare and eventually the bedroom games that they had only heard snippets of information about from adult conversations overheard. Ms. Heath's nostalgia transformed into a horrified worry about Nawiri discovery of such games and was relieved with the knowledge of Momma Kiesha's highly anticipated return in August. It was just too much stress having two 'in like' teenagers under one roof.

Besides graduation day, Junior prom was one of the most exciting days of middle school. For just one day, the children could dress up and pretend to be grown-ups. Young Kings and Queens in all their glory. Sasha and Nawiri had just completed a raw food detox diet that her mother suggested, to give them the perfect form and attitude for the big day. The girls' excitement had even infected Devontae, more than anything he just wanted to see Nawiri in her olive green dress. He imagined that she would resemble a young Naomi Campbell, dressed for the runway or a movie premier. The anticipation was more than he could handle, finding himself debilitated and sleeping most of the day while Sasha and Nawiri did their hair, polished their finger nails and toes, and put on the finishing touches of glitter and their mothers' sweet smelling perfumes. They ran around the upstairs of the house, back and forth between the bathroom and Nawiri's bedroom.

Ms. Karena, Ms. Robyn and Ms. Heath had given up their efforts to help with the prom preparations, realizing that their daughters already knew exactly what they needed and didn't need them to help turn those dreams into realities. The mothers sat in the living room drinking herbal green tea and discussing current events. Sade was playing on the stereo, drowning out the sound of Nawiri and Sasha's footsteps above them.

'There have been so many children killed this summer. Already two got shot in my neighborhood last week! I'm just sick of it, when is the madness gonna stop?' asked Ms. Karena.

'Mmm mmm mmm, I don't even know. My heart goes out to the families. I like to think that things are unfolding as they should but some things just don't seem right, you know?' Ms. Heath shook her head.

'Yes Momma Heath, I know.'

'Let me go check on Devontae. I haven't heard a peep out of him all day and they only have about thirty minutes until we need to start taking pictures and then get them over to the dance hall.'

'Alright, I'll go check on the girls' progress,' said Ms. Karena, 'Robyn, you coming?'

'Yup, I'll be right up, let me turn down this music.'

Ms. Heath knocked on Devontae's door but there was no answer. Knocked twice, three times, nothing. Then, she tried the handle and the door was unlocked. The living room area was dim with the exception of the sunlight flooding through the window blinds, casting artistic shapes on the walls. Flashes of light were broken up by the shadows of hard objects. Devontae lie fast asleep on the couch with an open book over his face. She chuckled to herself and knelt over to shake him.

'Huh? What? Cambria, stop shaking me!'

Devontae looked up and saw the magnificent face that he had grown to love as a Great Aunt or perhaps a Grandmother-in-Law.

'It's not Cambria, it's me, Ms. Heath. Wake up darling, you only have a half hour to get ready.'

'Aww man, I don't know what happened! One minute, I was awake and the next I was gone.'

'It's ok, just hurry.'

Ms. Heath exited his apartment, her floral summer dress trailing her as she rushed to the ringing kitchen phone.

'Hello,' she gasped, 'You're there? Perfect timing, I'll be there to pick you up in ten minutes!'

Devontae jumped in the shower and jumped back out with the same quickness. Reached for deodorant and knocked over the lotion. Fumbled for socks and got a wooden splinter caught in his finger from the dresser, then stubbed his toe on the closet door frame as he walked into the light to remove the splinter. Hopping around the room, he finally collapsed onto the bed and starred at the ceiling. Rushing was giving him a great deal of difficulty but more than anything he was pained because two of the most important women in his life would not be there to see him dressed in a suit, with one of the most beautiful and intelligent girls in school on his arm. He imagined how his mother's face would just light up with joy, her left dimple in plain view for all to see her brilliant smile and glowing pride. He pulled out the splinter and continued to dress more carefully. Another knock at the door came as he was tying his shoes. It was Ms. Heath again; she had come to retrieve him for pictures.

'The girls are all ready and Sasha's date is here too. Are you ready dear?'

'Yes, ma'am, I just need to grab the flowers I bought for Nawiri.'

Devontae re-adjusted his tie one last time, took up the flowers from the table and headed out of the door. As soon as he turned toward the stairs to walk down, he caught a glimpse of a familiar figure in his peripheral vision and looked up to see his mother looking healthier than he had ever seen her, smiling exactly how he had imagined.

'Momma!' Devontae exclaimed, running down the stairs to greet her. The embrace was well overdue, now much taller than she, the side of her face smooshed against her sons chest. Against her wishes, her eyes welled up with tears. Her heart full of pride and joy.

‘Ok, ok, you’re gonna squeeze the life outta me boy! When you get so big? My baby done gon’ and had a huge growth spurt. Look at you, so handsome. You know you get those good looks from me, right?!’

‘I know Momma, I know,’ Devontae smiled and put his arm around her shoulder as they walked to the front of the house where everyone else was waiting for them.

‘How did you get here?’

‘I took the bus.’

‘They let you go?’

‘Just for one day, I’m going back in the morning.’

‘O, ok.’

In the front of the house, Sasha and Nawiri held hands, posed for pictures and waited for Devontae to join them. He was the missing link to the dynamic trio. They were a group of three that had managed to see past material things and peered into one another’s hearts, finding solace and creating irreplaceable friendships. Devontae’s eyes fell on Nawiri just as she turned to meet his gaze. He closed his eyes and re-opened them just to make sure that he had truly seen the girl of his dreams. Indeed, it was she, in the flesh. As did she look upon him in disbelief. And indeed, it was he, in the flesh. They stood paralyzed; smiling at one another as if the rest of the world had melted away.

‘Well, are ya’ll gonna take some pictures or what? We just can’t stand around staring at each other all day,’ laughed Momma Kiesha.

Devontae shook his head and went to stand by the girls and Andrew, Sasha's date. They took so many pictures that their faces became sore from grinning. Devontae whispered to Nawiri, 'So, I think I'm ready to be in a relationship now.'

Nawiri looked at him. It was sure to be a lovely candid shot. 'I dunno, I think I wanna wait until next school year. Tenth grade, when we're sixteen, seems like a more appropriate time to start a relationship,' Nawiri said, winking at him. Yet, another picture perfect shot.

Devontae laughed, 'Ok, ok. Fair enough.'

Their mothers stood, holding hands, watching the children converse amongst themselves. They were stunned by their beauty and the positive essence that they created.

'We done well,' said Ms. Heath. 'Second that!' chorused Momma Keisha and Ms. Robyn. 'Third that!' exclaimed Ms. Karena.

Devontae looked over at them, remembering how they had been the first day they met and marveling at how far they had come. Still wishing Cambria was there to fix his cuff links and make fun of his appearance. 'Love you sis,' he mumbled to himself. 'What'd you say?' asked Nawiri. 'Nothin,' he smiled and touched her hand lightly. In no time, the Mercedes was zooming down Gloucester Drive to a Junior Prom that they would never forget.

I USED TO LOVE HIM

She ran as far as she could before she needed to stop. The projects were now barely visible in the distance, at least four blocks away. The surrounding houses did not belong to anyone she knew but she needed to get to a phone, immediately. She walked up to a man, who was washing his car, and asked to use the phone. He looked distrusting but she made up a story about how she was lost, trying to find a friend's house and just needed to clarify the directions. The man agreed reluctantly and hovered over her to make sure she was telling the truth and to prevent her from running off with his house phone. She looked up at him, annoyed, 'Do you really think I'm going to steal this old, spin dial, land line phone? Please, I would rather walk around with a five pound cell phone.' He loosened up and went to sit in the living room as she made her call in the kitchen. 'Hello? Hello? Red! I need you to come pick me up baby.'

'Who is this?'

'Whatchu mean, who is this? This is Cambria, nigga. Who else would it be?'

‘Oh my bad baby girl, I didn’t recognize the number. I’m busy right now, where you at?’

‘I’m using some random guy’s phone but you can pick me up at the bus stop on the corner of Outer Drive and Lahser? Hurry, please. If you don’t come, I won’t have anywhere else to go.’

‘Alright shit, you callin’ me like I don’t have shit else to do. I’ll be there as soon as I can.’

He hung up the phone abruptly and she thanked the man sitting in the living room and walked back outside, headed toward Outer Drive. Thinking about the speech her mother had just given brought tears to her eyes. She didn’t want to be away from them; even her mother’s irresponsibility wasn’t enough to make her hate her. She just wasn’t ready for change. It was too abrupt. Her mother had given her only one week to cope with the loss of the freedom she had grown so comfortable with.

‘What is she thinking? How selfish is it to abandon your kids for drugs and then abandon them again for rehab? Who the hell is this lady? She don’t know me. How is she gonna act like my Momma? I’m my own Momma. Shit, my own Daddy, too. These women really think they gon’ just fill in? Where the fuck did they even come from? One minute they sittin’ on the front porch, laughin’ it up, the next minute they trynna take over my life. What the hell did I do to deserve this? I just want my family, not some made up family, patched together with some outsiders acting like the glue. One whole year wit’ strangers – hell to the naw. Fuck all that. Red’ll take care of me. I hope. Man, I hope this nigga will. Otherwise, I don't know who to turn to. Momma just put her trust in anybody. She should be doin' background checks and shit. How do she know these women not just trynna steal her kids away from her like the government?'

Cambria made it to the bus stop and waited for three hours until Red pulled up, the smell of reefer travelled with bellows of smoke coming out of his cracked windows. She opened the door and observed him before sitting down in the passenger seat. 'What took you so fuckin' long?'

'Don't ask questions, just shut the door.' Before she could fully close the door, he had already sped off, running red lights and stop signs. Cambria loved the exhilaration that came with riding in his car. She just shut her eyes and let the flashes of light streak by. On the freeway, she felt like she was flying. Above the entire world, above all of the problems. Free from pain, heartache, and suffering. They drove on for hours and she fell asleep gripping the seat belt tightly.

The weeks went by slowly. There was nothing much to do but cook and watch television. Red told her not to leave the apartment when he was gone, which was usually three or four days at a time. So, Cambria drew on her imagination and memories of the past. She enjoyed painting the most. Images of her family filled the pages of her sketch pad as she was determined not to forget the precious moments they shared. When painting became dull, she cooked the most elaborate meals. First, she followed directions given on the Food Network; then, she moved on to making her own experiments, which evolved into masterpieces most of the time. Red could always smell the food brewing when he was approaching the apartment and his stomach growled as he opened the door and watched his now seventeen year old chef goddess putting the finishing touches on his meal.

'Hey Baby, look what I made! It's basil-orange pineapple chicken with red potatoes and I got a mixed salad over there on the counter.'

He sat on the couch smiling, 'I don't know why I ain't steal you away before this! I ain't never ate so good in my life. My baby can cook!'

'Mmhmm, but you know Red, I'm kinda ready to go back to school. I want to start again next school year; I feel like an old person sitting around in this house all day. I've been trying to occupy myself, I even read now like my little brother but it's not enough. I want to be a normal teenager with friends and homework.'

'Well, you shouldn't have run away. I need you to hold this spot down now. You a integral part of my life and my operations, you wanna just up and leave me?'

'No,' Cambria frowned, 'I don't think going to school will take me away from you. You not even here half the time.'

'Oh, I'm not here? So, you saying I don't treat you good? You sayin' Daddy don't do enough for you? I'm out here in these streets hustlin' so that YOU can have a place to live bitch and listen to your ungrateful ass!' He stood up and towered over her, 'Say you love me.'

'No, I'm angry right now!'

Red's face tightened so much that his jaw locked in place and he could feel his teeth grinding. Then, he raised his hand and slapped her across the face with the back of his hand. She raised her head, her eyes pleading for him to stop. He grabbed her throat and threw her down to the floor.

'Are you ready to say it now?'

'No!'

He kicked her in the stomach and asked again. 'I love you,' she whispered.

Cambria wondered what would become of her, she had refused to live with Ms. Heath for the fear of losing control of her life and now her confidence and independence were being taken from her by the same person that had once made her feel so free. Red looked down at her and smiled, 'That's what I thought. You wouldn't be shit without me, just remember that. If you leave, there's nothing out there in the world for you. You'll end up just like yo' strung out Momma.' Red ate a piece of the chicken with his hand and continued to speak as she lay speechless on the floor, 'Get up and finish gettin' this food ready. I gotta meet with my boss outside real quick. This shit better be on the table and ready to eat by the time I get back in here.'

Cambria could hear faint voices in the hallway. Perhaps it was curiosity or maybe just an urge to disobey his orders but Cambria stood, looked at the unprepared table and walked in the opposite direction toward the door. She cracked it slightly, so that she could hear the conversation more clearly.

'What's up man?' asked Red.

'Nothing much, how is everything running?'

'Smooth, smooth, everything's good.'

'I heard there were some problems on Elm Street, has that been taken care of?'

'Of course man, the day after the drop, we mirked the three niggas involved, clean. Everybody else knows what it is but you know every once in a while somebody try to boss up.'

'Alright, so if I hear anything else about it, then I'll know you didn't complete the job, right? I don't want to have to dust off your unfinished business again like six months ago with that little nigga Young John or whatever they called him.'

'Man, if it wasn't good, then I would tell you but I promise everything is good, I was just over there today and we got some young, eager motherfuckers out there, ready to die for the team.'

'That's what's up, so can I come in? Is there a reason you got me standing in the hallway like this?'

'Oh man, my bitch in there cooking dinner right now. Plus, I just figured we would just talk for a few minutes, my bad Mr. Simmons, next time I'll make sure she cooks enough for three.'

Cambria winced, the name sounded so familiar. 'Simmons,' she thought, 'that is the same last name as the girl Devontae and the twins are living with. Could he be her father?'

'Who is that?' asked Mr. Simmons, as he stared at four fingers wrapped around Red's apartment door. Cambria tried to shut the door softly but it was too late, Red had heard the click of the lock snapping back into place. She looked around for something to protect herself and ran to the kitchen, grabbing for the sharpest knife she could find. Hiding in the pantry, she awaited his return nervously knowing that she had heard way more information than she was supposed to. She had been away from home for so long that she didn't even know that Young John was dead and thought about how devastated Devontae was or if he even knew himself. Her brother's childhood best friend killed by his girlfriend's dad. She stood in shock and fear for her own life.

Back in the hallway, Red exclaimed, 'I'm sorry man, I'll make sure I teach her a lesson.'

'No, but you fucked up because you said my name. Did you tell her who I was?'

'I said I was going to talk to my boss but she don't really know shit.'

'Is that so? A lot of incriminating words were just spoken; I don't think I need to say anything more, you know what you have to do.'

'But come on man, she's just a kid.'

‘There are no exceptions in this business. You make mistakes like a man and you fix them like a man. And make sure my money is in the safety deposit box by Monday. I got islands to buy and political guests to entertain.’ Mr. Simmons walked to the elevator and waited silently, no longer acknowledging Red’s presence.

Time stood still as each second expanded its breadth within the stale, humid hall. The earth stopped rotating and even the wind seemed to be holding its movement anticipating evil to surface. The fragile lives that rule the world were confronted with their power and their vulnerability, simultaneously. Their control over the moment and lack of control over life. The paradoxical existence of man was on the cusp of an explosion, where parallel realities collided, unexpectedly. Street life versus elite life; childhood versus adulthood; healing versus hurting; life versus death. When Red’s hand touched the door knob it burned like hell from electrostatic charges or from a fire on the other side of the door. He hoped it was a fire. Looking over his shoulder, he saw Mr. Simmons disappear into the elevator. Then, he was left alone to suffer with his own conscience and a deafening silence.

‘Damn Cambria, I didn’t wanna have to do this to you. Why did she have to be so nosey? Everything woulda been cool. I mighta even let her ass go back to school. This is some cold-blooded shit I’m about to do.’ Opening the door, he could see that the table was not made like he had asked her to do. The lettuce and sliced apples had begun to turn brown. This added fuel to the fire in his eyes and momentum to his deadly stride. He cocked his gun, screwed on the silencer and waited for the sound of movement.

Cambria stood as still as she possibly could, holding her breath for twenty seconds at a time. She couldn't hear Red but she knew he was in the apartment, hovering like a black alley cat, thirsty for blood like a lion. She could sense his intentions. Time passed slowly as they each waited for the other to make a move. After what felt like an hour, Red finally broke; he began to search the cabinets and closets. Now, in front of the pantry, he reached for the handle but was too slow, Cambria burst through the doors, hitting him in the head and thrust the kitchen knife into his upper chest, he staggered backwards, caught his balance and began to advance toward her, raising his gun to her back as she ran. The click was so faint even Cambria did not hear it. She fell to the ground, just as she reached the front door. Heaving and sighing, she fought for each breath, hoping that it wouldn't be her last. There were no sounds from the other end of the apartment after the thump from Red's large body hitting the floor. Listening intently, she hoisted herself up again, reaching her hand out for the door knob. She fell to the ground, managing to open it slightly. Then she began to dream a thousand dreams of the past, present and future, slowly as if each second in time was elapsing one million times slower than the tick of a second hand. Visions of bus stops, snicker bars and sneaky neighbors, two girls and a little boy turned to darkness as she closed her aching eyes. Waiting for the sound of ambulance sirens.

As Mr. Simmons exited the building, a blind old man seated in a dingy lawn chair looked over at him and said intently, 'Your time is coming.' Mr. Simmons was not sure who it was intended for, so he said thank you absentmindedly, slid into his Bentley and drove away. He shook his head and focused on the road ahead, determined to ignore the signs.

27153118R00148

Made in the USA
Lexington, KY
29 October 2013